Dear Margaret,

By Pamela Ackerson

Julia,
Never Forget,

Pamela Acke[rson]

Praise For the Wilderness Series

Across the Wilderness

I ended up reading this book in one day! It has everything I love - suspense, romance, and history - all wrapped into one. -- Nikki

Pamela Ackerson has put a human face on that struggle in a very creative way that allows the reader to have their feet in both the past and present. Highly recommend! - Frank

I like stories which engage my imagination in this way and this one kept me wondering. I kept wondering when and where she would wake up and what adventures and challenges she would face next. And that for me, was fun. - Debra Parmley (Award-winning author)

Excellent ebook and I would recommend this ebook to one and all. Will look forward to reading more from this author. I give this ebook a five star rating. - Amazon Reader

Very interesting book lots of history once started could not put down until finished so much history and suspense really enjoyable – Shirley

Excellent! Along with the adventure & romance was history. The history of our Native Americans and how they were treated is so very sad. Ms. Ackerson wove the threads of this story into a beautiful tale. Can't wait to read her next one. - Patty

Into the Wilderness

I will read this story over again often, you can count on that. - Ruby

Love the twists that occur in this book, amazing sequel... - Amazon Reader

If you enjoy time-travel, you'll enjoy this. Very clever and fun to read. −Amazon Reader

Wonderfully written... Couldn't put it down, I want more. I hope it goes on and on. Thank you for the love!!!! – G. Mort

Wilderness Bound

The author does have a good writing style and that brings this book to a four star rating. – P.S. Winn

Excellent! I hate that I'm ready to read the last book of the series, I hate to see it end! I love this story very much! – Ruby Slippers

Warriors of the Wilderness

I love these stories and can hardly wait for the fifth book! Wonderful job with this series! – Ruby Slippers

Books by Pamela Ackerson

The Wilderness Series
Across the Wilderness
Into the Wilderness
Wilderness Bound
Warriors of the Wilderness
Out of the Wilderness

Dear Margaret,

A Granny Pants Story   (New Series of Children's Stories)
The Long and Little Doggie
Riley Gets into Predicaments
Available in Spanish
El Perrito Largo y el Perrito Pequeno (La Serie del Perrito Largo y Pequeno)

Non-Fiction:
*I Was Just a Radioman (*The Memoirs of a Pearl Harbor Survivor, Black Cat, and decorated war veteran.)

Dear Margaret,

Pamela Ackerson

© Pamela Ackerson 2016

Edited by: Chrissy Szarek

Disclaimer:

This is a work of fiction based on the real life experiences of
Henry P. Lawrence, a Pearl Harbor survivor, Black Cat, and
decorated World War II veteran

Summer 1940

Dear Harry,

I'm so glad we decided to write to each other while you're away with the Reserves. I wasn't sure what kind of books you like to read so I packed a couple for you.

Even though you'll only be gone for a few weeks, I'm glad we exchanged addresses.

I know you'll be busy and may not have time to write to me. I would love to hear about your experiences and travels.

Best Regards,
Margaret

Letter One

Summer 1940

Dear Margaret,

This may not get mailed out as quickly as I would like, so it may be a bit of a long letter. Let me tell you how this all came about…

In June of 1940, my brother, Don, and I joined the Ninth Division, US Naval Reserve Unit at the State Armory on Thames Street in Newport. All of our drills were held at the Armory on Wednesday evenings.

We were required to march in uniform and with a rifle. We had lessons on seamanship, and classes in the rate we'd be striking. I was assigned to be a fireman striker, and Don was assigned a seaman striker. If you don't already know, a striker in the Navy is like a person working as an apprentice.

The qualifications for a fireman striker consisted of knowing Navy seamanship, and the fireman rate. Included classes on all type of Navy knots, flags, oil fired engines, and anything else that had to be known about running the power plant of ships.

This all started because of my older brother Mark's brilliant idea for me to join before I turned eighteen. He talked Don (who was eighteen) and me into joining the Reserves. "It'd be great extra money…" he said. His famous saying, "if there's to be a war, we'd probably be doing mine sweeping duty on the East Coast."

At the time we signed up for the Reserves, Mark, who was also attached to our unit, had already been called up for active duty.

Anyway, that's Mark for you.

At our first drill session, we were issued a full sea bag of US Navy clothing consisting of blues, whites, dungarees, hats, underwear, hammock with blankets, and other miscellaneous items. Everything had to be stenciled with our name or initials, and they also had to be rolled according to the Navy Blue Jacket Manual.

While most of my friends were playing at Easton's Beach, my brother and I continued with our training. In the summer of 1940, most of our unit who hadn't been called to active duty went on a two week cruise aboard the USS Williams (DD108). This ship was an old four stacker, which didn't have very many modern conveniences and was mainly used to train US Reserves.

We went aboard the USS Williams on July 24, 1940. I was assigned to the fire gang, and Don was topside with the seamen.

Just so you know, when I told my parents I wanted to be a fireman, this isn't what I was talking about.

I was stationed in the fireroom with two other men. Our work schedule when we were underway was four hours on and eight hours off.

While underway, we manned the oil burners and made sure that we were creating enough steam pressure. When the guys in the engine room requested more pressure for more speed, or whatever, we had to ensure that it was there for them.

If we had the wrong mix of oil and air, it would create a lot of black smoke, and they'd alert us by banging on the deck.

Upon my very first shift, I knew immediately why we worked in the fireroom for only four hours. The heat down there was extreme, sweat dripped down our faces, pouring out of every pore on our bodies. It soaked our clothing until we could practically wring a bucket of water out of the uniforms.

Taking salt pills was a necessity, unless we wanted to end up out cold and face first on the floor of the ship. As for ventilation, the air coming from topside was very limited. When we were through with our shift, we'd take a quick shower, fresh water was at a premium, and our time was limited.

During those two weeks, we sailed from Newport Harbor to Norfolk, VA for mine sweeping exercises. I could hear Mark's voice in my head. "See, I told you that you'd be doing mine sweeping duty on the East Coast."

3

Dear Margaret,

At Norfolk we boarded an old Eagle Boat built by Ford that they used in WWI. It was set up with a fish, a buoy-type canister shaped like a fish. The fish would be dragged through the water by a cable attached to the ship. The cable had cutters on it. When it would catch a mine cable, it'd be able to cut through the cable and the mine would surface. We continuously launched the fish until everyone was proficient in its capabilities. (Some cutters had small explosive charges.)

Lunch on board, cold cuts slapped between two pieces of bread, what the Navy calls an H C sandwich. It didn't turn out too well for a few of the men. They got sick, possibly from the sandwiches so we secured for the day, leaving Hampton Roads and returned to the USS Williams.

We traveled at night from Norfolk, and ran into a storm on Chesapeake Bay. I was on duty in the fireroom at the time. The ship was actually leaving the water and we could feel it shake, grinding, and screaming on its return to the water. We held on to anything that would keep us from falling; the storm had taken control of the ship.

When I got off duty, I looked around for my brother, Don. Going topside you could see the storm had caused some damage to the ship. When I found Don on the topside, he'd said it'd been pretty bad.

During the two weeks aboard the USS Williams, we were given liberty in Washington, DC. I saw the Capital and a few other tourist attractions.

My pay for the two weeks was $9.80. At seventeen, I was making darn good money. It wasn't too bad at all. The pay for recruits, at that time, was $21.00 a month.

Our tour will end August 9, 1940.

Mid-Summer 1940

Dear Harry,

I'm so glad you were able to find the time to write over summer vacation. I guess it wasn't much of break for you and time got away from both of us when school started this year.

It's a good thing you gave me the address when you did. That's twice you've had good timing! At least we got to have some fun at the dance last week.

It was such a surprise to return to school and find out you were gone so soon. I'm looking forward to keeping in touch.

Not much is happening here, just sleepy Newport as always. Keeping myself occupied, I'm working part-time at LaForge and volunteering with the Red Cross.

School is school. However, I am looking forward to getting my senior pictures done over the summer and getting ready for my senior year. Gee, I thought it would never get here!

Although, I know you'll be busy I really enjoyed receiving your letter while you were away and would love to hear more about your experiences and travels. I understand that it'll all be kind of technical, but tell me anyway, even if it does sound like you're just outlining your days.

Best Regards,
Margaret

Dear Margaret,

Letter Two

Spring 1941

Dear Margaret,

My senior year flew by so fast. Between Reserves and school, I was keeping pretty busy. I'm guessing it'll be the same for you when you start your senior year in September.

I'm sure you already know this, but after we returned from our cruise, more and more men were being activated. Under a lend-lease program created by President Roosevelt and Congress the USS Williams was traded to England in a fifty ship deal for bases in the Atlantic.

On May 12, 1941 our unit was called to active duty. (I'm sure you saw it in the Newport Daily News.) As you know, I was in my senior year at Rogers. I was so close to graduation. Oh well, there was nothing I could do to change the orders. I'd signed up in the Reserves and that's the way it goes.

Our unit reported to the US Naval Training Station in Newport, RI for boot training.

Chief Houghton was our leading chief for the seven weeks we were there. At boot camp our unit was integrated with the reserve unit from Pawtucket, RI. At the station, we had to complete the full requirement of boot training.

We reported to Barracks D and were confined in the detention area for the first two weeks. After detention, we moved to Barracks A. Once we were in the barracks, we were free to go about the base. The Navy kept us pretty busy, but we were still able to have liberty on the weekends. I made a quick stop home and took off to shoot the bull with our friends before heading back.

For our training with firearms, our unit went to the Navy shooting range at Third Beach where we learned how to handle the 303 rifle and the BAR rifle. The BAR is an automatic rifle that's not quite a traditional rifle but not quite a machine gun either. With the Browning automatic rifle, it's possible to either shoot off a single shot or select the full automatic firing mode. We had to do both. It was quite an experience. We also went out to the skeet range and shot birds (disks).

Every Friday we have full inspection of our gear and barracks. On Saturdays, all units march in front of the Naval War College. As all the units march off the field, they play The Beer Barrel Polka.

One day after a march, we returned to our barracks and Chief Houghton told us that we were supposed to sing along with the band. On the following Saturday, we sang loud and clear.

He was happy.

It's kind of a big deal, so I'm going to brag a bit. We also won the right to fly the best unit flag. The best unit flag is awarded weekly.

The USS Constellation was docked at the pier for two nights. Our unit stayed aboard for both nights. Sleeping accommodations were in our hammock below deck. Matter of fact, it was the first time I used a hammock. We're required to carry it with us whenever we travel.

You probably know some of the people or their families attached to our unit: my brother Don, Chris Hayes, Jack Noonan, Tony Sundell, Lester McCoy, and Michael Jacobs.

Of course, there were others, but these were the guys I have contact with as my time in the service continues.

It's been a busy few weeks.

Looking forward to hearing from you.

Best Regards,
Harry

P.S. I was going to send this out when the orders arrived. So, I slipped it in.

Don and Chris were sent to NAS Jacksonville, FL to attend Aviation Metalsmith School. Jack, Tony, Lester, Michael, and a

Dear Margaret,

few from the Pawtucket unit (can't recall their names) and I was sent to Aviation Radio School at NAS Sand Point in Seattle, WA.

Summer 1941

Dear Harry,

Hope all is going well over there in Seattle and it's not raining too much.

Thank you for writing me. I enjoy hearing about everything you've been doing.

You've been busy!

My uncle said that Sand Point will be a main NAS in the Pacific if we end up in the war. I asked him about the radio school there, too. He said you'd be learning Morse code. And, he said you might even have to learn secret codes to transmit to our ships and aviation pilots.

That is so killer-diller!

It must've been really scary to shoot that automatic rifle.

I've never shot a gun before. My girlfriend, Kay, and I were talking about it and we decided to see if our parents will let us go skeet shooting or perhaps even let us shoot real guns at the target range in Portsmouth.

But, I have to wait. They're mad at me right now. After the dance on Saturday, a group of us went downtown. We were having so much fun, we just didn't want it to end.

My oldest sister was in the bar having drinks with her friend and told me to scram or she'd tell Mom. Well, she told on me anyway—said I was hanging with a bunch of Khaki wacky girls. Not true, only Jan is and even she's just all talk and no action.

Oh well, can't complain too much. They're letting me go to the beach dance next week.

Take care of yourself.

Best Regards,
Margaret

Letter Three

August 1941

Dear Margaret,

I finally got to Sand Point NAS. It was a long and interesting trip to get here. No commercial flights for us, we had to take a train.

On June 24th, we left Newport in an open stake body truck. There were a lot of people there to see us off and say our good-byes. My sister Mary and my mother were among the well-wishers.

We boarded a train in Melville that took us to Providence, and then on to New York.

In New York, we boarded a Pullman train that brought us to Seattle. It took three days to go cross-country with stops at Chicago and Denver.

When we arrived in Seattle, we were transported to NAS Sand Point. We arrived just in time to start classes the first of July. The Aviation Radio School was new and we were the second class to attend.

Your uncle was right on target. Aviation Radio classes consisted of learning how to type at least 40 wpm, take and receive Morse code at 30 wpm or higher, semaphore (flags), blinker (flashing light) and we had to learn how to fire up radio gear being used in naval aviation.

I think typing without looking at the keys is the biggest challenge for me. Although, Morse code, along with specific code words, is like learning another language.

We've got Saturday leave and we're going to check out some joints and shoot the bull with our new mates. Then back to the grindstone, memorizing all the blinkers, signals, and flags.

I need to practice my speed with tapping in the Morse codes, too. I'm a little slow on that, and being who I am, I have to give my best.

I'll put this in the mail for now.

Hope you're enjoying your summer.

Best Regards,
Harry

End of summer 1941

Dear Harry,

I've had a busy summer, getting ready for senior year, swimming at Easton's Beach, work at the restaurant, and volunteering at the Red Cross.

Our family was invited to go to Bailey's Beach for a party. Being a private party with all the ritzy rich, was a gas. We had to have a special invitation to attend. Not that we're rich, or anything like that, but my mother's family came from money before the depression and they kindly still invite her to many of their parties.

There was so much food there! I ate so much BBQ and burgers, I was stuffed for days. Drinks flowed like water. The band was killer-diller and we danced all day and night. Oh, how I love to swing and foxtrot.

Everyone's talking about the war heating up in Europe now that Germany, Italy, and Romania have declared war on the Soviet Union. Finland's joined the bandwagon, too. What is wrong with these people? Putting J's on Jewish passports, making them wear Jewish stars to identify them and massacring them!

I just want to yell at the world and tell all of them to stop.

I pray for our boys in Europe and am glad you're on the Pacific coast away from all of that.

I know it'll be hard for you to write and I look forward to hearing from you.

Best Regards,
Margaret

Letter Four

Early December 1941

Dear Margaret,

Sorry, it took so long to get a letter to you. By now you should be started in your senior year at Rogers. I hope you have a great year, one you'll always look back on with a smile.

So much went on in the last few months. I haven't forgotten you. I've just been keeping my nose to the grindstone. There was a lot to learn and I wanted to do my best.

And it *was* a grind, but I succeeded and graduated on October 24th. Our weekends were normally our own, but I took that time to study up until this point. After I was more confident in my codes and signals I started to relax a little.

A group of us took a bus to Seattle for liberty. Seattle's a very clean city and the people were hospitable. In Seattle, I saw my first college football game and I saw Count Basie at one of the theaters. It was as you say, "Killer-diller."

Of course I didn't go on liberty every weekend, only when I had money.

On November 3rd, we left Seattle by train for my next duty station... Hawaii. We arrived on the 4th at Mare Island, a naval base in San Pablo Bay north of San Francisco, and stayed overnight.

We were transported by a stack body truck to San Francisco to meet with the USS Downes (DD375), USS Cassin (DD372), and USS Shaw (DD373) which were waiting to take us to the Hawaiian Islands.

On November 12th, we sailed for Hawaii and arrived on November 19th. While on board the USS Downes, I was assigned as a messenger on the bridge.

After our arrival at Pearl Harbor we were taken by whale boat to Ford Island. My orders were that I was assigned to VP 22, Jack Noonan was also assigned to VP 22. I think you know his younger sister.

They dropped us off at the barracks which was facing the harbor. It was a beautiful view with most of the battleships tied up at buoys alongside of the island. The barracks were quite empty at the time because the squadron was away at Midway.

Our sleeping quarters were on the second floor and the mess hall was on the first floor. We had to check in to our squadron each morning. Jack and I were assigned to the radio shack and were kept busy doing multiple assignments.

My first holiday in the Navy was Thanksgiving. We had the day off. The Thanksgiving meal was a dinner to remember.

Before I joined the Naval Reserves, the farthest I was away from home (without my parents) was a couple of summer vacations in Taunton on my cousin's farm. I'd made a couple of day trips to Uxbridge and also went to visit my brother Vic, who was living on Long Island.

Now, I find myself six thousand miles away from home. It just seems odd. Home is so very far away.

While on liberty, we hit a couple of joints, got to know some of the locals, and enjoyed their company.

I wasn't very lonesome. I think the regimentation in the service helped a lot, letters from home, and just having fun, keeping busy. Jack and I were together a lot which also helped. He's a hot-ticker, I'll tell you what. He's made it easier to be away from friends and family.

As I go along with this writing, I find that the service is a very funny place. In a way, I get to know a lot of people, but don't really know them that well.

The place filled up pretty quick when the squadron that was at Midway returned December 5th.

Well, the plane's going out today so, I'll put this in the mail.

Best Regards,
Harry

December 1941

Dear Harry,

Holy Cow!

By the time I got your letter, the 7th had already passed. I hope you get this. I saw your mom and Mary the other day and they said you were fine. Of course, they worry about you. Your mom must've been terrified.

What a mess. After hearing about the attack on Pearl Harbor and the U.S. Philippines, the country is up in arms.

We were just finished with Sunday dinner and Uncle Popeye asked if he could turn on the radio. My sisters and I were cleaning away the dishes while mom was storing the left-overs in the icebox.

We stared at the radio with our mouths hanging open. None of us wanted to believe it. It couldn't be true. The Japanese couldn't be that stupid to attack *us*—attack Hawaii, an American territory.

That whole day was surreal. All I could think of was you, and all our friends, hoping you were safe. Praying that you'd survived the attack.

My heart still clenches thinking about it.

Everyone is signing up to join the service. Men and some women are still waiting in line for hours to serve our country. I guess MacArthur's Air Force got hit pretty badly when the Japs bombed the airfields in the Philippines.

We heard on the news that Great Britain declared war on Japan on the same day America did. We listened to the president's speech the day after Pearl Harbor was attacked. Some of the kids at school said that he's using Al Capone's bullet-proof car.

Everyone is trying to do their part for the country. They're talking about potential food rationing, and collecting scrap metal and aluminum.

There's already a bunch of gobbledygook going around

which I try to ignore. I imagine it'll get worse, along with the propaganda that goes with it all.

I know you won't have much free time, especially now, so write when you can.

Where were you when all of this happened? What'd you do when you realized the Japs were attacking the base?

I'll be here, doing what I can on my end. Be careful.

Best Regards,
Margaret

Letter Five

Late night December 7, 1941

Dear Margaret,

December 7th started like any other Sunday in the service for me. Since it was my day off, I slept in, which means I didn't have any breakfast. I was planning on going to a later mass at the Chapel and wanted to have a lazy day, have a quick lunch afterwards, and shoot the bull with the guys.

I remember being slightly aggravated because there was so much noise and I was being rudely awakened from a wonderfully sound sleep.

Well, everything seemed muffled at first. Then, as I started to awaken, I heard was a lot of noise, explosions. I practically fell out of bed, and I jumped up to see what was going on. As I was running toward the window, someone yelled that we were being attacked by the Japs.

You have to understand, all of this took seconds, split seconds that seemed to be in slow motion—watching a train wreck that can't be stopped. Every second's engraved in my eyes and brain as each movement was pulling me forward.

I ran to the balcony in my shorts where I had an excellent view of the harbor. The unmistakable sound of multiple airplane bombers coming at us thundered in my ears.

Looking up, I could see large formations of aircraft going to other targets. I looked over the harbor, and the Jap torpedo planes and dive bombers had a nice clean run at the Battleships.

Watching them drop torpedoes and bombs, I could feel the percussion of the explosions as they annihilated everything on Battleship row.

Some of the men on the ships were firing back, but it was a losing battle. Without any opposition, the Japs had everything going their way.

It was damned sad.

The clear air over the harbor was now encompassed with smoke, and the clean water turned black with oil.

Those of us in the barracks knew we had to get down to the squadron and report in. I don't remember when I grabbed my clothes, or how I managed to dress while I was watching the destruction unfold before my eyes.

As I slipped in my shoes, a bright flash blinded me. Looking over toward Battleship Row, flames were licking the oil in the harbor.

Just about that time there was another large explosion and I could see the USS Arizona was on fire. The black smoke from her went straight up into the sky. The Battleships tied up at Ford Island were settling to the bottom.

Our squadron was about a half-mile from the barracks. On our way down the road leading to our squadron we had to duck for cover a few times. After the Japs dropped their bombs they started strafing, shooting at us as we hightailed it to the hanger.

Someone would yell and we'd hit the dirt. You could see them coming with their guns firing, but we all reported in without anyone getting hit.

The dry docks across the harbor from our barracks were in flames. I hadn't known it then, but the USS Downes was one of the ships that was hit. (The Downes was in dry dock at the time Pearl was bombed.)

Our squadron and all the planes we'd parked two days ago were destroyed. The hanger we shared with VP21 had a couple of large gaping holes.

Since we were still under attack, the strafing aircraft kept us moving as quickly as possible. We had to get the burning planes away from the ones that *weren't* on fire.

All of a sudden, it was dead silent. There was an eerie stillness, a numbness after hearing all the explosions. I stopped for a moment, looking around the harbor. All I could see was burning ships. There were a lot of small whale boats and fishing boats picking up men from the oil blackened water.

The smell was something I don't think I'll ever forget. The

stench of burning oil and destruction…

Someone from our squadron suggested to me to set up a fifty caliber machine gun in one of the PBY's. He asked if I ever shot one and I said no.

I learned real quick.

We moved the PBY over to the opening of the hanger, positioning it so we could shoot and protect the airplane as much as possible.

We ended up relieving each other, taking turns being on look-out, etc. I was on the ground after we loaded the machine gun.

Just about then the Japs returned. This time they were doing a lot more strafing. When the planes started coming in our direction, we started firing the fifty that we'd just loaded.

How a handful of seconds could feel like eternity, I don't know. But it sure felt like eternity to me. All I could do was stand near the opening of the hanger, watch, and point to any aircraft coming our way.

I'll tell you right now, when they came back the second time around, anyone that had a gun was firing it.

During all this mess, the USS Nevada which had gotten up steam was coming up the channel, ran itself into a sandbar in the middle of the harbor on purpose. I think they did it so the ship wouldn't sink in the harbor, and foul up the channel.

When the strafing ended, they mentioned the men from the ships would be needing clothing. I left the squadron area and went up to the barracks to open my locker.

For some reason or other I went through the mess hall.

That was a huge mistake. Margaret, I just can't seem to get this out of my head.

Every table had a body on it. They were all covered with oil and blood. The medics were working as fast as they could to help the wounded and relieve their pain. Seeing this, watching the medics, kicked in the reality of what was happening around me.

I swear I started sweating it out right there.

I ran to my locker, bringing back everything to the squadron that I could spare. Handing them to the guy who was collecting the items for the sailors, I turned to the squadron leader for more direction.

He had everyone moving planes around and cleaning up the hanger. We broke out the thirty and fifty caliber ammo, and started linking them in belts so we'd be ready when they came back. Most of us couldn't believe how old the ammo was (WW1), and we all hoped they would work.

Our ships were gone!

All the ships that'd been tied up at Ford Island were on the bottom of the harbor or close to it. Men were putting out the fires, and starting the pumps to get the water out. Taking inventory of what happened on Ford Island, the Japs knocked out all our Battleships, and two of them went belly up.

Over in the dry dock area, billowing smoke was visible, from the ships that were hit. The USS Arizona was still smoking, its forward mast was starting to bend because of the intense heat.

It was a complete loss.

The fishing and whale boats from the island residents were still cruising the harbor, trying to save whoever was left, picking up bodies, and taking pictures.

All three PBY squadrons VP22, 23, and 24 lost most of their planes. My squadron, the VP22 didn't have any planes that were able to fly. All three squadrons were crippled.

The Japs had hit outside of the hanger we shared with VP 21, and also disabled all of our planes on the ramp. We had nothing left and would have to wait for replacements from the States, for planes and ships to be built before we could defend ourselves.

Time was a factor we couldn't control.

The day went by pretty fast, they kept us busy doing a little of this and that. When evening rolled around we ate some dry sandwiches. So much had happened that it wasn't until then I realized I hadn't eaten all day. Dry as they were, those sandwiches tasted good.

They mentioned there was a water truck on the strip so Red (Jack Noonan) and I went looking. As we were out on the strip, with a blink of an eye, the sky lit up with gunfire.

There was a spattering of gunfire everywhere, all day, and I think I was finally scared. I don't think I had time to be scared earlier that morning. There was no time to think, just time to do.

Red and I couldn't find the water tank. We had to beat it back to the squadron area once the gunfire had started again.

We found out later a few of our own planes were trying to land at Ford.

It was pretty late by this time and the word came down that we might as well turn in for the night.

It was a long day, and I'm sure this letter has been quite a read for you. Thanks for keeping in touch.

Best Regards,
Harry

Letter Six

Mid-December 1941

Dear Margaret,

Well, I never got the other letter out in time, so I'm putting them both together. I hope you don't mind.

Mail was delayed and I'm not sure if you've sent another letter yet. So, I'm just going to continue telling you about Pearl.

Now that it's been a few days since the attack, everything seems to have started to sink in. There's a pall over the area that none of us can let go of.

I have so many unanswered questions.

The day after the Japs bombed us, actually the next morning, I didn't know where we were going to eat. They said the mess hall was open so we headed down there.

I couldn't believe my eyes. Everything was clean. I had to take a few moments, to adjust to the memory of the wounded men and using the very same table to chow down.

It was like I never saw all those sailors and medics—like they'd never even been there.

However, after breakfast I looked out over the harbor, and saw the mess the attack had created. The perpetual knot in my stomach rebelled. The smell still blanketed the area and would for a long time, a continuous reminder of what the Japs had done.

Reality was back.

They already had work crews working on the ships. Water was pumped out of the ships, and men were working with torches, working at a maddening pace to get everything literally shipshape again.

At the time of the Pearl Harbor attack, we did an assessment of damages. We had ninety-six ships on battleship row. Eighteen of them were sunk and seriously damaged. Eight Battleships-gone!

Almost 1300 injured men! I'm shaking my head thinking about the mess hall. The count of the dead so far is over 2400. How is it that I survived when so many—so many will never go home?

We didn't have any aircraft that wasn't damaged somehow. I think they said 350 were destroyed or damaged. If the Japs' goal was to destroy our military presence in the Pacific, they came darn close to it.

My head spins, my heart clenches, and my stomach feels like it's had a perpetual knot in it. It's a good thing I don't have time to think.

It's been a few days since the Japs bombed Pearl and they're letting us go into (Honolulu) so we could send telegrams home to let our families know we're all right.

So, you get a bonus, two letters in one.

Best Regards,
Harry

January 1942

Dear Harry,

It's been a crazy few weeks here. I've dropped out of school, doing everything I can with the Red Cross, and working full-time at La Forge.

My mother's now working at the shipyards—the Torpedo Station on Goat Island. She twisted her ankle the other day, running to catch the ferry. Not sure how she did it, but the way she was describing it, she made a mad-dashing leap off the dock, across the water. She hurt herself when she landed on the ferry deck.

She worked like that all day Friday, stayed on the couch over the weekend, then went right back to work on Monday. Normally, she volunteers at the Navy hospital on the base but had to bow out this past weekend. (She was a nurse before she married and had us.)

My mother and the three of us kids are all doing something, either with the hospital or Red Cross. Everything we can for our boys fighting for our country!

It's crazy everything you've been dealing with. I can't imagine what's going through your mind, and the tragedies you've seen. When you were telling me about the attack on Pearl Harbor and everything you had to do, you sounded so detached, as if you had to distance yourself from what happened. I imagine that this is all so overwhelming and you're doing what needs to be done, regardless of how remote it seems to me.

I'm glad you're writing to me, letting me know what's happening over there. Please keep, writing. I love hearing from you. And stay safe!

Best Regards,
Margaret

Letter Seven

February 1942

Dear Margaret,

I hope your mom is doing better. I could just picture her doing a flying leap to grab that ferry so she wouldn't be late for work. Your mom's a feisty one, as you well know.

Days off have been few and far between. I've taken to getting dance lessons at the NCO rec hall. When I get home I'll be the best ducky shin-cracker around.

To our pleasant surprise, within a couple of weeks of the attack on Pearl, replacement planes started arriving. Boy, we sure were relieved to see them.

I was assigned to ground crew before they put me on a flight crew.

The PBY-5 Catalinas are flying boats. Once they arrived, we launched and recovered aircraft when they returned from their schedule flight.

On launch, we have to take off the two side wheels and the rear wheel while the aircraft's in the water with their engines idling. When they return we put the wheels back on, and the recovery vessel takes them from the boat ramp to their parking area or the hanger.

I was put on a flight crew as a second radioman for about a week, then assigned to pull mess duty. The squadron pulled out while I was on mess duty for the South Pacific (Dutch East Indies).

After mess duty I was put on a flight crew again, as second radioman and started drawing flight skins. That means I'll get a 50% increase in pay.

Dear Margaret,

About this time, we were all issued gas masks which we had to carry with us at all times. The gas mask unit was in a blue bag with a shoulder strap. It's very bulky, and they're a pain in the neck.

Can't remember if I told you before, but I was assigned to VP22 in November and have now been transferred to VP 24.

They've got me scheduled for a Pat Wing Two Radio School which I'll be starting soon.

I'm off for now, duty calls.

Thank you for keeping in touch. I look forward to hearing from you.

Best Regards,
Harry

April 1942

Dear Harry,

I hope this letter finds you happy and healthy.

I think it's exciting that you'll be doing so much flying. I imagine all the Radio School you're going to entails more memorization, new codes, and a quick thinking mind. They must be happy with you and your work.

The Naval Training Station here has a constant flow of young men. Weekends are a complete influx of all military servicemen from here to Quonset Point and Melville. Newport is obviously the place for sailors and such to go.

My mother won't let us go downtown or anywhere anymore. It doesn't matter at this point. It's too cold, snowy, and I don't have the time to go to the White Horse Tavern anyway which is usually where we go.

Don't know how much information you're getting about what's going on in the states. Santa Barbara, California was hit by a Japanese submarine. They shelled an oil refinery, Richfield Oil. It's scary thinking about it. Between the Germans attacking us on the Atlantic side and the Japanese on the Pacific side, there's so much to worry about.

On a happier note, our family went out to Island Park on Sunday to celebrate my sister's birthday.

And of course, we had to go to Flo's!

I can't believe my sister's twenty-one. I can't wait until I turn eighteen! Twenty-one seems so far away.

Do you have clams and steamers there? I imagine being on an island you can get lots of seafood.

I packed you up some books and such. It should be coming to you soon. My Uncle Popeye said the letters get there faster than the packages. I wasn't sure what type of books you like to read so I put in *The Citadel* by Cronin, *For Whom the Bell Tolls* by Hemingway, and a few comic books that my cousin gave me to send you. (*Captain America*).

Dear Margaret,

If you let me know what kind of books you like, I can send more. And if there's anything else you would like? Some peppermints or Goo Goo Clusters? I remember you saying you like them. Not sure how melted the clusters would be but if you'd like some, I'll pack them up in the next care package.

Well, got to go to work.

Be safe!

Best Regards,
Margaret

Letter Eight

April 1942

Dear Margaret,

Thank you for the package. I enjoy reading science fiction and mystery, so you were right on target there.

I can understand why your parents don't want you down at the wharfs on the weekends right now. Not that I'd say you were in danger, but there's some hot-blooded, hard-boiled, boys out there looking for a good time.

You're right. Nobody does it like Flo's. Her clam cakes will never be beat!

There are a lot of different types of seafood here. Although, they don't have steamers, not many people even know what they are. There's no sight of *chourico* or *linquica*, either. Oh well, I'll fill up on all of that when I get home.

I entered Pat Wing Two Radio School in March, and, if all goes well, will graduate in May. It's a constant deluge of new words, distinctions, and codes. The hardest part is that there's a lot of stuff we can't take out of the classroom, and we're not allowed to write anything down. We have to learn it all right there.

I imagine it'll be an ongoing thing since the Japs have a way of breaking our codes. We'll be learning new stuff all the time.

This school's about the same as the one in Seattle, but they're pushing some pretty heavy training on the equipment we'll be using in the PBY's.

The PBY's will be used to destroy enemy submarines, Jap supply ships, aircraft carriers, etc. And since they can fly long distances, they'll be used for long-range recon trips, search, air,

Dear Margaret,

and sea rescue.

I'm going to send this off for now. I've got a couple other letters to write to my parents and family.
Thank you for keeping in touch.

Best Regards,
Harry

May 1942

Dear Harry

The snows have melted. The freezing weather is gone. Shorts are out of the chest and I'm loving the great weather. Can't go to the beach like I used to, but I guess sooner or later it was going to happen.

Work is work. I mean how much can I say about waitressing? LaForge is a great place to work, no complaints. I've been delivering meals with my friend Nancy to the elderly. They need so much help. I wish I could do more.

They've started rationing sugar and petrol. My parents hardly ever use the car anyway. I think the only time my uncle uses it is when he has to go to Boston or Providence for work.

Now that the ground is thawing, people are coming out of their houses. Everyone is getting ready for the tourist season which has started a bit on the late side this year.

Doris Duke came into town for a visit with one of her friends. We went to lunch the other day. We've been friends for a couple years now, and she always makes sure to stop by and see me.

She said she wouldn't be staying at Rough Point for the summer and was heading to Europe. I tried talking her out of it. It's too dangerous for her to be traveling around all over Europe right now. Doris seems to think there won't be a problem. Said I was a big worry-wart.

She did give me a Paris address to use to write her but said that it'd be rare that she'd be staying there. I know she's a big girl, but she's a good friend and I do worry.

Everyone's extremely upset about the surrender on Bataan. The news is saying that Major General King surrendered his army to the Japanese, about 76,000 men. Holy smokes! What's going to happen to those men?

I don't even want to imagine what they'll do. The Japanese don't exactly have a very good reputation for taking care of prisoners. How are they going to feed all those men? I don't even want to think about what *our* men are going to go through in one of their POW camps!

I don't know if this bothers me or not. I understand but also, don't. They're putting Japanese-Americans in internment camps, no matter how much Japanese blood they have or how many generations that they've been here.

But yet, according to the newspapers, we've got over 10,000 Japanese-American men fighting for us. I bet they have to try ten times harder than any other soldier—just to prove they're willing to die for the U.S.

I can't wait for this war to be over and you can come home. So all of our men can come home! Please, take care.

Best Regards,
Margaret

Letter Nine

June 1942

Dear Margaret,

I promise to try my best to not become a POW!

I don't think your friend should be going to Europe right now either. But, she's a grown woman and knows what she wants. Most likely, it isn't safe to be traveling anywhere at this point.

It doesn't really get cold here. It's the perfect temperature for me. I miss my home and family but I don't miss the cold and snow. Nope, you can have it. Hawaii, when it comes down to the weather, has spoiled me.

After radio school, I was sent to Pat Wing One Gunnery School at Kaneohe Bay from May to June. It was quite an extensive course.

Day 1—bomb and torpedo racks.

Day 2—sighting and recognition's of enemy aircraft and ships.

Day 3 & 4—strip and learn all about 30cal and 50cal machine guns, and they also threw in small arms. I was qualified to wear a machine gunners patch!

The squadron has advanced duty bases at Midway and also Johnston Island. No flight log book, no recording of time flew; most of our flights were patrols.

We had a hurricane flight in which we flew right through the eye and out the other side. It was a pretty rough ride.

I remember staring at the walls of the plane wondering if the hurricane force winds would rip us apart. The plane shook like we were a box being kicked down the street. I kept picturing (like the cartoons and funny papers), the rivets working their way out and pinging me in the head.

I completely understand what people mean when they say a white-knuckled moment.

While at school half of VP24 was sent to Midway. The rest of us, including me, were put on stand-by They're calling it the Battle of Midway which happened in the early part of June, the 3-6th.

After school in June, I was put on another flight crew. PBY radio equipment consisted of two radio receivers (RU1) which had removable coils that gave you access to the frequency you needed.

A frequency meter lined up the correct frequency. The radio transmitter (GO9), and a directional radio antenna has to be turned by hand.

The antenna's on the wing between the two engines. The radio and transmitter antenna's strung from one wing to the tail and other wing with a lead in between the wing to tail to our radio station.

There's also a trailing wire antenna that we had to set up. Here you'd have to take out a shut off assembly that went to the bottom of the aircraft, and put in the trailing wire assemble into the pipe tube.

We also have a voice receiver/transmitter that the pilot uses when he's in range for landing and takeoff. (Distance was line of sight or a little better)

My duties as a radioman are pretty straight forward. A radioman assures all radio equipment's operable. After takeoff, we report that we were airborne. When on patrol we send CW signal in Morse code to let them know we were airborne.

We're required to stand watch on that frequency, and also set up the other receiver to listen for emergency signals. Also, we have to listen in on the intercom if we were needed.

Intercom and emergency frequency in one ear, and frequency watch in the other. It took a little while to get used to, but if anything came in from the base you would normally cut off the other two. This way you could keep your full attention on receiving Morse code.

I know I'm getting technical. I'm completely fascinated by

all this and it's coming out in my letters to you. Sorry, I'm getting as bad as my brother!

I think it helps me think all of this through. With all the recon we've been doing, and runs it all seems to blend together.

Well, I'm back. Although, I'm sure you didn't notice. Silly thing to write but this is the first chance I've had to pick up a pen without detailing events in the flight log.

It's been a little over a week. We were called out on a Dumbo run and things haven't stopped since. And we've just been called again.

I'm send this out for now before it takes another week or so to get back to you. Take care. Thanks for writing. I really appreciate hearing from you.

Best Regards,
Harry

Dear Margaret,

July 1942

Dear Harry,

Hope all is going well on your end.

I have to ask, what's a Dumbo run?

Everyone was so excited when we heard the news about the Midway Battle. What a great victory for the U.S. They're saying that the Navy broke the Japs code and was able to turn the planned ambush around to *our* benefit. The newspapers are all bragging about how it's turned the war around.

Killer-diller!

I cannot believe you actually flew one of those planes into a hurricane. Have you forgotten what the '38 hurricane did to Newport? And your plane flew into one? And through the eye of the storm, too?

I would've been shaking in my boots, crying my eyes out! I haven't forgotten the howling winds, tornadoes, crashing trees, flooded streets, and leveled houses. The tidal wave that destroyed Easton's Beach is more than enough of a reminder about how dangerous hurricanes are. There's something wrong with someone who willingly flies into a hurricane.

Oh dear, I guess I shouldn't have written that!

You must have a *lot* of trust in your pilot. But come to think of it, I guess you really didn't *have* much of a choice, did you?

We went to Somerset to visit my Uncle Popeye and Aunt Alice over the Fourth of July holiday.

I know I've mentioned him before, and yes, that's what we call him. Let me tell you why.

He had eye surgery done years ago. It was experimental and they used a cat eye as a transplant. Not sure exactly what they used, or what they did—I just know it was from a cat.

So, his left eye is squinted and he looks like Popeye.

And he smokes a pipe, has a tattoo on his arm, has a cleft in his chin, and used to be an officer in the Navy, and was a sailor…

And Aunt Alice is a skinny-Minnie, too!

I'm sure you can now understand why he's Uncle Popeye.

Aren't families wonderful? There's so many awesome stories that people have. Got any from your side of the family?

Time for me to head out to do some Red Cross distribution and then I'm off work at LaForge.

Stay safe.

Best Regards,
Margaret

Letter Ten

End of August 1942

Dear Margaret,

Wow, sounds like you have the real Popeye as an uncle. When I get back, I have got to meet him.

Sorry, I haven't written sooner. We've been a bit busy.

A Dumbo run is an air-rescue flight. If a ship's in distress, or possibly a downed plane and crew, we search for the survivors, and bring them back to safety. Sometimes, we're being shot at, sometimes, it's an easy run.

I saw my brother, Mark, the first time since I left home June 15, 1942. We went on Liberty and he also gave me a tour of his ship, the USS San Diego. The San Diego was just commissioned, and she's got all modern equipment on it.

It really was great. We always have fun together and enjoy each other's company.

Since I've been with the VP24, I've flown about three hundred hours as 2nd Radioman, so far. We had a two week tour at Midway in early July, from the 5th through the 17th.

When we got there, they still hadn't done any repairs to the island. The Japs had completely demolished everything on the ground. They'd just put up tents for our living quarters, and as far as the mess hall was concerned, they cooked everything out in the open in large pots.

They issued us our own eating gear metal folded plate, a metal cup with water canteen, and silverware. After we finished eating we had to wash our gear in large heated fifty gallon drums of hot water.

No water for showers so most of us used the ocean for our

bathing with salt water soap.

The latrines were plain holes in the ground with a couple of boards so you could sit down. Like camping out, definitely a bit on the primitive side.

As far as recreation was concerned, we played with the Gooney Birds (Albatross). We'd capture one and swing it to see if we could get it to fly. Most of the time, they'd fall flat on their face. Such fun with the birds. They may not know how to land, but they sure know how to fall without getting hurt!

Watching the Gooney Birds was a riot. We laughed so hard watching some of them land, the muscles on my sides hurt the next day. They're huge, so graceful flying in the air, and then, when they go to land all that gracefulness? Poof! Gone! I about busted a gut laughing.

They'd put their feet out to land and tumble onto the ground in every which way, head over tails, flapping, and gawking loudly. I'm surprised they didn't break their necks or wings. Some of them would just stop and lay there after they tumbled all over the place.

Unfortunately, they were a hazard for our planes. Especially on landing and take-off; a couple of our planes had been hit, and they'd make a large dent on the aircraft leading edge. Which, of course, happened to us. It put the aircraft out of service until it was fixed.

Most of our patrols were ten hour hops. On one patrol we took a couple of Marines with us and they enjoyed the ride very much. They'd sit in the blister where the gunner sits, and stand our watches. I got friendly with this one sergeant, and saw him one time later in one of the bars in town.

I was sitting having a drink and this marine who just came from the states started giving me a hard time. The sergeant saw what was going on and told the kid to take off. I wish I could remember the sergeant's name, but I do remember he was with the first division.

I heard later that he was shipped to the Canal (Guadalcanal) in the Solomon Islands with the First Marine Division. They've been doing a series of air, ground, and sea actions. I hope he's safe.

Since we don't stay on any particular island for very long, when we were returned to Ford Island they gave us R&R at the

Royal Hawaiian Hotel. Boy, this was really great! The price on the door for that room was $110. Can you imagine?

We had a room shared with a buddy. The eating facilities were memorable. The dining room had a beautiful view of Waikiki beach, and if you wanted to go swimming all you had to do was go out the back door and you'd be in the ocean. The beach was very flat and it was a long walk in the water to get over my head.

Now, you asked about family stuff. My sister's fiancé, Van is in the Navy and has received a few medals. Do you recall the USS Squalus submarine disaster? He was one of the divers who used the Momsen Lung to save the survivors. I believe he received the Navy Cross for his service.

He's talked about it a couple of times. I'd sit there enthralled listening to his stories, especially that one. I can't imagine diving 250 feet. Van doesn't grandstand or anything like that. Just talks about it, like it was all part of the job.

Everything else is pretty mundane. My parents came to the U.S. from the Azores, and settled in Newport. My brother, Jack, is the only one who was born in the Azores, all the rest of us kids were born in Newport.

My mom has a college education and is fluent in three languages. Pop barely speaks English and works as a gardener and, of course, at the garage that they own. Both are smart as a whip.

I spoke Portuguese until I started kindergarten. I knew a little English, enough to get by. Pop doesn't speak English very well, so if we want to have a lengthy conversation with him, we speak Portuguese. He can get by though, get his message across when he needs to.

We have a rule in the house. When we're home, we can speak Portuguese. But, we speak English outside of the house. Mom always says that it's rude to speak Portuguese when the people around don't understand what's being said.

Her biggest reason was that we're Americans now, we speak English.

Like my mother, I'm good with languages. I got A's in French class, too.

Perhaps that's why I do so well with the radio codes? Who knows?

Well, I think I've bored you enough. Keep writing. I love hearing from you.

Best Regards,
Harry

September 1942

Dear Harry,

Well, summer is done. The tourists are gone and work has slowed to a dead crawl. Newport has rolled up its streets until Memorial Day weekend.

I haven't heard from my friend, Doris. I hope she's safe.

I do remember the Squalus. It was one of the submarines they'd built in Portsmouth. We lost a lot of good men in that test dive. I'm amazed that people can go that deep. Your future brother-in-law is killer-diller!

My Uncle Popeye was a diver in the Navy before he retired. I wonder if he knows any of the men from the Squalus. I'll have to ask.

The summer was filled with news of the war. Not sure how much information you're getting or if you're getting anything at all.

All the newspapers wrote about the Midway battle, the Bataan Death March, and the bombing in Tokyo. But you probably already know all of that stuff. Are you hearing much about Hitler and the war in Europe?

There's a thing called O.S.S. now where the U.S. has spies working for them. It's called the Office of Strategic Services and they do covert operations and gather any intelligence information overseas.

We had a scrap metal and scrap rubber drive a couple of times this summer. A few threats and a couple black-out drills. My mom hung a service flag in the window; the one with eight stars to represent the 8 million Americans who are serving overseas.

My cousin Mary, is now a WAAC (Women's Army Auxiliary Corps), not sure where she's going but she stopped by to say good-bye before she left to go overseas. She said she'd be doing non-combat duties.

I'm out of work for a few days. I sliced my finger with a

scalpel trying to get some metal out of a patient. Just a few stitches, nothing to complain about. Don't know what I was thinking, allowing myself to get distracted. A nurse came in the room to get something out of one of the drawers and instead of ignoring her, I looked up and boom! Oh well.

I'm off for now, Mom's calling.

Please be careful.

Best Regards,
Margaret

Dear Margaret,

Letter Eleven

October 1942

Dear Margaret

Hope all is well on your side of the world. Keep those fingers safe. No more stitches allowed! You're lucky it wasn't worse, I'm glad that it was minor.

Thank you very much for the birthday card and book!

When's your birthday?

I hadn't heard about the Bataan Death March. With a name like that I'm not sure I want to know. Honestly, we're aren't hearing anything about what's going on in the rest of the world. A few things here and there, some rumors—some not.

There's not a lot of information about the Atlantic war or any U.S. current events coming to us at all. If we hear anything it's from new recruits coming in and telling us what's going on or letters from home.

On September 4th to the 14th, we had a two week tour at Johnson Island. Just about the time the Air Force made a PR bombing run to Wake Island.

We were sent out from Johnson Island to a point that would give the Air Force a CW signal so they would know where they were if they lost their bearing. A CW signal is a continuous wave radar.

After this tour we had R&R again at the Royal Hawaiian. We had a bunch of fun, shooting the bull, playing around. It was definitely needed. Once that was done, everyone was ready to get back to work.

Most of our flights out of Ford Island are patrols and practice landings. On one of the patrols, we had a fire in the electrical junction box in the radio compartment.

I opened the box and the fire was starting to reach for the overhead.

We started emptying CO_2 bottles to keep the fire down. I put all the switches on the junction box to the off position hoping it'd help. After that, I disconnected the DC Battery which was under the radio seat hoping again with everything off that the fire would expend itself.

After the fire burned itself out, we found one of the relays in the box had shorted, which caused the fire. We headed back to base without any more problems.

I was scared. If the fire had gotten out of control, it would've gone up to the wings where our gas tanks were.

If that had happened, it would've been "goodbye".

Flying with VP24, all our aircraft were PBY 5s. The only thing new that was added to the aircraft was RADAR and an IFF box.

The RADAR didn't work well as the antenna was a bunch of sticks attached to the bow of the aircraft with antenna wire strung across these sticks.

They also installed a friend or foe box (IFF) which sent out a signal to let them know we weren't the enemy.

Last but not least, we're seaplanes, and had to land in the channel of Pearl Harbor. When we approached our landing ramp a crew was sent out to attach portable wheels; one on each side of the aircraft and one in the rear.

Once the wheels are attached, a tow truck pulls us up the ramp tail first, and parks the aircraft. We enter and exit from the blister.

It's time consuming and probably the reason they had transferred all squadrons (seaplane) on Ford Island to Kaneohe Bay. The harbor was getting very busy with ships coming in and out.

I'm no longer with VP 24. I was with 24 from February to September. I have no idea how many flights we went on. I didn't record any of it.

The squadron received the Presidential Unit Citation. Also, I made 3rd class petty officer while assigned to this squadron.

I've got classes I need to attend to learn new codes, another round of memorization. We can't let up—at all. We have to stay

Dear Margaret,

ahead of the Japs!

Best Regards,
Harry

End of November 1942

Dear Harry

Sorry, this is going to be a long letter! I'm not normally a big letter writer (as you can tell by my other letters) but there's a lot to tell for a change.

Congratulations on the promotion and the Presidential Unit Citation. I asked Uncle Popeye about it and he said that it's issued to men who perform outstanding acts of courage and determination in missions that were under extremely dangerous situations.

That is so killer-diller!

Why aren't you with VP24 anymore? Does that mean you won't be flying the PBYs?

I'd be terrified to fly in an airplane. Isn't it scary? I don't know how you do it.

How was your Thanksgiving? Mine was the usual group for us. About twenty people came to the house bringing a favorite dish. We ate so much good food.

We did something different this year for our prayer before the meal. Usually, Uncle Popeye says the blessing but this time, Mom had everyone at the table give a special thanks to someone they know who is fighting the war or needs our prayers. It was a special moment for everyone. I asked that you return to us safely and soon.

My friend, Nancy and I went to the picture show the other night to see Casablanca starring Humphrey Bogart and Ingrid Bergman. We ended up leaving before it was over. I'm not a bluenose or anything like that but there was a bunch of fat-heads there, being loud and rude, so we left before trouble started. They probably had too much hooch.

And trouble did start, too. I heard a few days later that the owners of the Opera House called the police on them.

It's still playing so we'll probably try again this weekend.

I received a letter from Doris. It was post-marked from

Egypt. She asked if I'd been by Rough Point. I don't know why she'd think I'd go over there. She's not there, so I didn't see any need. But, I rode my bicycle by there just so I could tell her that it looked good.

She's doing well and working as a waitress! Can you picture the richest woman in the world waitressing? I can't. I just can't see it.

She didn't mention her husband, or why she's in Egypt. Who knows, that's Doris!

I'm curious. Do they let you celebrate the holidays? I've got a package coming for you for Christmas. Your mom and sister gave me ideas on what to get you. I hope you love it!

The newspapers have been covering the battles in Guadalcanal and the Solomon Islands. That's where you said your friend was shipped to, right? I'll keep him in my prayers.

There was a huge fire at a nightclub in Boston. Almost 500 people were killed. So very sad. It was supposed to be a night of fun.

I don't know how much you like science. My Uncle Popeye is a science buff. Loves reading up on rockets and all sorts of stuff. Ever since they launched that liquid fuel rocket in Massachusetts, he's been reading everything he can about it.

I was only a couple of years old when that happened, but he's talked about it so many times. I think he wants to build one! Last year, for Christmas, I bought him *A Method of Reaching Extreme Altitudes* by Robert Goddard. It's all about rockets and all that stuff.

He said that a few weeks ago, they were testing atoms for a chain reaction in Illinois, energy from an atomic nucleus, and if it worked that there'd be an unlimited source of power for us. Can you imagine?

I have an odd question. I was re-reading your last letter and I realized I was hearing your voice speaking to me as I was reading it. Do you hear my voice when you read my letters?

Oh, and I know you didn't ask for it, but I've enclosed a picture.

Have a great holiday Harry, and stay safe.

Best Regards,
Margaret

Letter Twelve

Mid-December 1942

Dear Margaret

Your letter came fast this time. You must've had good timing. I think that's a great idea that your family did for Thanksgiving. It's something that makes people think about how blessed they really are.

I don't really think about flying. I just do it. My mind isn't on flying anyway, there's so much other stuff I'm concentrating on.

I re-read your letters, too. And yes, I hear your voice when I'm reading them. Thank you for the picture! Everybody keeps teasing me about what a Sheba you are.

I'm cooking with gas! And they're jealous.

I've enclosed a recent picture of me.

We haven't had a lot of spare time but we were able to sit down to a nice Thanksgiving meal. It was some good cooking.

My oldest brother loves science, rockets, etc. and I remember he was always talking about Goddard. Once he starts talking nuclei and rocket fuel, he just doesn't stop. I find it interesting but my brother will get very technical.

Keep your eyes open for the post man. I've sent you a package. I hope you like it.

When VP24 was transferred to Kaneohe, I was transferred to HEDRON FAW 2 last September and am expected to be there until next June.

While I'm with HEDRON, I'll be checking out as 1st Radioman in PBYs, PB2Ys, PBMs, and PB4Ys (B24s). The PB4Ys isn't a seaplane. I'll also have to work on small types of aircraft.

And just so you understand, I don't fly the planes, I'm a radioman—just a radioman. Although, I've been crossed trained in gunnery and can work in the blister if needed.

A few months ago, I had to go back and learn more codes. Japs keep breaking them. We have to stay ahead of the game.

I felt a bit out of place. I swear I was the only one in the group that was not an Indian.

It's been extremely busy the last few months, a lot of flights, night and day.

We've had a few headaches with the PBYs right now. They're always having generator trouble. Usually the planes will take off early in the morning, before the sun rises. They'd call us, and we'd have to go fix the generator.

There are two things that we could do depending on the type of problem. We could take the generator out or fix the clutch which would slip. This meant we'd have to set up the portable staging, and take the small cowling off the engine so we could get to it.

We'd have them start the engine again, and we'd sit on the staging, and adjust the clutch. It got easier after a while—after you got over the fear of falling off this small staging which was actually attached to the engine.

Other times if the engine wouldn't start we'd have to get up on the engine with a large crank and crank it until the engine started. The tricky part here was not to fall off the wing.

The propeller's turning, and you have to pull out the crank. (The crank's about three feet long) The worse part even with the engine idling was getting to the walkway which was between the two engines, and getting back down to the ground or the blister.

So far, I've put in about 90 hours in flying time since I've been with HEDRON FAW 2; some testing aircraft or flying so pilots could get their flight time in. It's been pretty hot fighting over here on the Pacific side, a few close calls but we're doing what we need to do.

Keep in touch. I love hearing from you.

Best Regards,
Harry

End of December 1942

Dear Harry,

Unfortunately, this will be a very short letter. Mom was injured at work (The Torpedo Station on Goat Island) and all my spare time is taking up the slack in the household.

A piece of metal flew into her eye and she had to go to the hospital. She's home, recuperating.

She was putting in a *lot* of hours. The Torpedo Station has been cranking out a huge amount of torpedoes and she'd been practically living there.

ON top of the fact that her eye is patched, she's having a hard time moving around. Mom's always been very active. She's not used to sitting around, and is getting antsy—doesn't know what to do with herself, or the extra time on her hands.

They aren't sure if she'll see out of that eye again. I guess, time will tell.

Christmas was celebrated at my aunt's house this year. They take turns, which seems fair to me. That way it's not always on just one person.

Thank you for the Hawaiian skirt! I absolutely *love* it. I hope you've received your gift by now and are enjoying it as well.

Sorry this is so short, I've got to run to the market.

Take care!

Best Regards,
Margaret

Dear Margaret,

Letter Thirteen

February 1943

Dear Margaret

Thank you for the card, sketch pad, and drawing pencils. They're great and I started using them right away. I apologize for not sending thanks sooner or even writing. It's crazy here.

I got a touch of malaria. Not sure which island I contracted it on. Nothing for you to worry about. I'm fine.

We hop from island to island and never stay on one for very long. Got to keep moving around so we won't be found.

I've gotten promoted to 2nd Radioman. Most of my flights have been on the PBY's but I'm still assigned to the flight crews on the other planes I mentioned before.

She also sent me clippings of Ma and other mothers in Newport who had four sons in the service. Mark, Don, and myself, are in the Navy. Hap (Jack) joined the Merchant Marine.

Ma also said that Don is home due to an injury.

You know Red (Jack Noonan). He had a tour of duty in the South Pacific and is back in the states.

I also saw Michael Jacobs who just completed a tour of the South Pacific. We had quite a bull session the night before he flew back to the States. His squadron left Kaneohe the next day and unfortunately the plane that Michael was on never made it back.

I'm glad I got to spend some time with him...

It takes approximately twenty hours of flying time to get back to the States. (California)

After that loss, the Navy stopped all squadrons from taking the PBY aircraft back. It's a long trip home even after the flight.

Once we arrive in California, we have to travel across the country to get back to Newport.

Victory at the Canal!

The battles at the Canal are pretty much over. The Japs have evacuated the island. I may have mentioned this before, I preferred the older PBY-5s, the weight of the gear in the 5A's are heavier, giving us less power and range. Some of VP-24 has been transferred to Espiritu Santo. I'm here at HEDRON FAW 2 doing Dumbo runs, night flights, bounces, and other assorted missions.

I know I'm being vague but, I'd just be repeating myself since I'm not really doing anything different than I have been.

I hope all is well. Best wishes for your mother to recuperate from her injury. I can't imagine how painful that was.

Take care.

Best Regards,
Harry

June 1943

Dear Harry,

Mom went back to work at the Torpedo Station a few weeks ago. There's permanent damage. We're grateful that she didn't lose complete sight. She's cranky, and I can completely understand. How hard it must be to have to readjust to something like that.

I saw your brother, Don, and your sister. He's doing better. He doesn't look very happy about being sent home after his injury. I can understand. I'm sure, once he's feeling better, he'll find something to do to help with the war effort.

I know this may be a silly question, but what exactly do Merchant Marines do?

I understand that you can't tell me everything that's going on over there. They have advertisements at the theatre and in the newspapers that warn to be careful with what we write and say. Careless talk can be pieced together by the enemy.

I read in the newspaper that they may have found a new penicillin. Isn't it amazing how far medicine has come? This is going to help so many people.

The president passed a law freezing wage and price increases. Coal miners have gone on strike. I understand they need to have more pay, and better working environment, but now isn't the time. I personally believe they're hurting the U.S. by striking. Perhaps it won't last long. Someone's got to bend.

I can't decide if the year is going by fast or dragging. It seems at the beginning of the year it was taking forever for each day to go by and then, boom, it's June!

Tourist season has started, but, it's not like before the war. I'd say about half the people are coming to the island. My summer hours at LaForge haven't increased and normally they've got me working more once school's out.

Nancy's boyfriend's back home on a thirty day leave. He was injured in North Africa fighting against the Germans

(General Rommel) and I guess they let him come home for a bit. He's heading back once his leave is up.

If you haven't heard about anything on the German side of the war, Rommel is a German general who they call the Desert Fox. He's been touted as being a genius at tank warfare. According to Nancy's boyfriend, Garrett, the fighting against Rommel's command has been pretty fierce.

Please take care.

Best Regards,
Margaret

Letter Fourteen

July 1943

Dear Margaret,

Sorry, it's been a really long time since I've written. I know you worry, and I apologize. The South Pacific is pretty hot right now and we've been quite busy.

To answer your question, I think the Merchant Marines get the wrong end of the deal and a lot less credit than they should. Almost everything we need arrives by ship, ships manned by the Merchant Marines. It is just as dangerous for them as it is for any of the other armed services.

Don't let anyone tell you differently. These men put their lives on the line every day. Many of the seamen are "too old" to join the regular armed services, don't have good hearing, or can't see that well—things that the armed services reject. So, some of them join the Merchant Marines.

As far as I know, their ships are not armed. If they're approached by enemy ships or planes, they have no way to defend themselves.

They're sitting ducks!

It takes a lot of courage to take to the seas during war time without being able to defend yourself against attacks. I imagine there are some who are captured, become POWs that we don't hear about.

A few weeks ago, I got myself assigned to VP71 as a 1st Radioman on a flight crew. I figured I was never going to get back to the states, and if I pulled a tour down south I would at least get leave.

I also had a choice to join a PBY4Y squadron, also known as B24s. I don't particularly care for this aircraft when I worked on them, and since they gave me a choice, I went with VP71.

We've got an incredible team. Lt. Cmdr. C.K. Harper, USN was made commanding officer of VP71 Nine crews made up the nucleus. Lt. Cmdr. Sears took the remaining crews to form VB104 a Navy liberator squadron that used the PBY4Ys.

We didn't train long at Kaneohe as most of our training was gunnery and bombing torpedo runs, including night water bounce, high altitude bombing at Lanai, and also checking out RADAR.

We were now flying PBY5c's which were a new series of seaplanes, equipped with a better RADAR antenna system, and one new radio receiver which was then called a super heterodyne (ARR 1).

Here's a bit of trivia for you. The PBYs were the first aircraft to use RADAR.

We didn't have to change coils with the new radio receiver; my second receiver was still the old type (RU1). Otherwise nothing else was new. We trained from June 12th to the 20th.

We left Kaneohe on 21st for Palmyra Atoll (Satapuala Base). We had to make a stop at Upolu Samoa (Western Samoa). The pitch control was giving us a problem, and we had to lay over for a replacement part. The pitch control is pretty important and we can't fly without it working properly.

The easiest way to explain is that there are three different types of motion that affects the airplane's center of gravity. Roll, pitch, and yaw.

One takes care of the front to back axis (roll), one takes care of the vertical axis (yaw), and then, the pitch takes care of the side-to-side axis.

All three have to be working properly in order for the plane to have the proper center of gravity.

Liberty was spent in Apia, Samoa; the island where Robert Louis Stevenson lived. The natives on the island still live in huts and are very friendly. I met a native who knew Stevenson, and we had quite a bull session.

After we fixed our aircraft, we caught up to the rest of the squadron in Espiritu Santo, New Hebrides Island. Then, on the 29th, we boarded the USS Curtiss (AV-4) which is a seaplane tender. It'll be our home base for a while.

Hope you're enjoying your summer. Write when you can, I

Dear Margaret,

love hearing from you.

Best Regards,
Harry

August 1943

Dear Harry,

I understand that it's hard for you to get mail out. I think the whole town waits for the post every day to hear from friends and loved ones. I stopped going to the armory to look at the list they post. I don't know how you deal with it, being in the thick of things.

I have a pretty good idea of what you mean when you say the South Pacific is pretty hot. It's all over the newspapers. I understand you can't or won't write the gory details, and I'm grateful for that. But, you're so nonchalant about so much of what you're doing. Like the plane not functioning. It's obvious you could've crashed and burned.

Or even about the fire in the junction box. Fire, in an airplane, where the only place you can bail is the ocean!

I worry about you. I can't imagine how your mother feels, wondering if one of her son's names will end up on the list.

I realize you're fighting a war, but I find it fascinating that you're going to all of these different places and meeting real natives.

Oh, to be able to travel!

I had to pull out the world map to look up Apia, Samoa and Espiritu Santo, New Hebrides Island. After looking on the map it makes me wonder, how in the world did Robert Louis Stevenson find Apia or anyone find these islands at all!

They're just these itsy bitsy little dots on the map. Uncle Popeye found Apia and then we found Espiritu from there.

It looks like you're close to Australia. Would you be able to go there on leave?

On the home front, there was a riot in Illinois where some people were killed. They were protesting Negroes taking away jobs from whites. I get that some people out of work don't want jobs taken away from them but, not sure why Negroes aren't supposed to be able to work and feed their families, too.

Dear Margaret,

There's rioting in New York, California, and Michigan, too. I guess Hitler-racism has become contagious here, creating a gang mentality. In California, they went after the Hispanics in zoot suits and Negroes.

The radio said that over 300,000 whites and Negroes had moved to Detroit to work in the war plants. They're all there to work for our country. The police used sub-machine guns on the whites to stop the rioting.

What's wrong with these people? We shouldn't be fighting against ourselves. I imagine that's exactly what Hitler wants, dissention and division amongst ourselves—an un-united United States.

Oh, well. Enough of that! You don't need to be hearing about all this negative stuff.

For more positive news, Mom painted a stone in our garden with a big V for Victory Garden. We've always had a small garden but the last two years we've doubled the size. Everything is rationed and we're re-using everything we possibly can, to the point where we've become quite adept at creating new ideas for old items.

They have a saying. "Use it up, wear it out, make it do, or do without." We're doing what we can!

Please stay safe. Write when you can.

Best Regards,
Margaret

Letter Fifteen

September 1943

Dear Margaret,

I hope all is well on your end of the world.

I understand my letters may sound unemotional or distant to you. I think, well besides not being an emotional person, I just do what has to be done. I don't think about how it makes me feel, or the danger I'm in.

It needs to be done. I do it. That simple.

A Victory Garden is a good idea. My parents have one, too. We're all using and re-using everything we can—just a necessity of the times I guess.

I don't think it's changed too much for my parents. Things tightened up during the depression, and they just kept being frugal. Or perhaps, they were already frugal, I just didn't notice since I was so young.

They've got their gardens (herbs and vegetables) and the grapevines. I remember when I was younger, Don and I would come home from school, and one of our chores was to smash the grapes with our feet (after they were thoroughly cleaned) so my mother and, my sister, Mary could make wine.

They'd spend days putting vegetables and fruits in canning jars, etc.

Ah, the memory of coming home to the smell of Portuguese sweet bread cooking in the oven!

I agree travelling all over the world would be fantastic—under different circumstances, of course. But, we do have a few precious moments when we can see and meet people from the different places we've been.

Not sure Australia will be in the cards right now. We'll see.

Dear Margaret,

We're doing a lot of patrols, hops, and Dumbo flights so I can't see leave happening any time soon.

On July 2nd, our first patrol, we were supposed to go to Vanikoro, which was an advanced base approximately 230 miles north of Espiritu. We never arrived there as our compasses weren't working properly. It was quite a while before we realized something was wrong.

Ens. Cocks asked me if I could do anything. The first thing I tried was our DF (Direction Finder) which was also out as it wouldn't give me a true north or south null indication. I tried RADAR next. This didn't work either, as we were too far out for long range search.

Just about this time someone spotted a DD (Destroyer) on patrol, and we hailed it. No one else in the crew could take blinker so I was stuck with trying to receive any messages that I would request from them. I have to say, the Signalman aboard this ship was very patient with me after he realized my ability in receiving blinker was very poor.

Talk about sweating it out. Trying to receive blinker at 1000 feet in the air from a ship that was bouncing around was quite a challenge!

We did get the information we were looking for, and as soon as we were headed in the right direction, I fired the DF up, sent the signal to Ens. Cocks, which was all we needed.

Usually patrols average around 10 hours, but this one lasted 14.4 hours. We were sweating the gas, wondering if we were going to ditch or not. As luck would have it, we landed safely back at Espiritu.

On the 4th of July, we transferred living quarters from the USS Curtiss to the USS Chandeleur (AV 10) which is also a seaplane tender.

Most of our patrols were pretty normal, but as far as living aboard tenders, it was crowded. The ship personnel didn't care for it much either. It was quite a disruption for them because they had to cater to us.

Anytime we had to go to our aircraft—which was tied up at buoys in the harbor—they'd have to break out the boat and take us to our plane. They also had to deliver gas to our aircraft and load any armament that we'd need for our hop the next day.

I guess I should give you a little information about our dress code while flying. The enlisted men all wear dungarees, chambray shirts, work boots, which we called boon-dockers, sailor hats, and Mae West's (inflatable life jackets). The officers wear their khaki clothes.

We no longer wear leather helmets and goggles with the advent of the glass blister on the PBY5 series and up. Also, we don't wear parachute harnesses as we never flew that high. Our normal flight height's about 1000 feet.

One other thing that I'd like to mention, is tying to a buoy. If I can do a bit of bragging, I like doing this. It's a bit of a challenge and have gotten pretty good at it.

First of all, I go to the front 30 caliber gun turret, open the top cover, climb out, and stand on the rail that's on the bow near the waterline.

Next, I open the anchor compartment and pull out the hook. The pilot locates the buoy that we need to tie up to. As we are going through the water the men in the blister would be putting sea anchors out (collapsible canvas buckets with no bottom) which create a drag.

My job is to hook a small eye on the concrete anchor. Once I accomplish this, I signal the pilot to cut the engines. Yes, the engines are running the whole time.

I then proceed, to pull the hook out and put the permanent tie line in the eye of the anchor.

It's a bit of a challenge but I've gotten pretty good at it.

I've been long-winded. Sorry. I try to write a little at a time and then send it off to you. If my letters seem slightly abrupt sometimes, that's why.

Take care.

Keep writing. It brightens my day when I get a letter from you.

Best Regards,
Harry

October 1943

Dear Harry,

There isn't a lot going on here. Just the same old stuff.

We painted Mom's bedroom a few weeks ago. I think I got more in my hair than on the walls.

She's thrilled. The neighbor had given us some left over paint and we mixed them together with another batch and got the color she wanted.

Now she's looking at the dining room and talking about stripping the wallpaper off and putting new paper up.

I learned how to surf at Easton's Beach this past summer. I don't know how they stay on those boards! Seconds after I'm standing, I'm in the water. It was killer-diller, though, and everyone busted a gut laughing at each other.

Not sure if you've heard any news about the Atlantic side of the war. Mussolini was arrested a few months ago, but we heard on the radio that the Nazis managed to free him.

However, the most recent good news is that there's a cease-fire in Italy!

I was telling my uncle about some of things you've mentioned in your letters, he said something about you being a Black Cat. What in the world is a Black Cat?!

I can't believe you climb out of the airplane like that when the engines are running. I'm such a chicken. I don't think I could do anything like that.

Actually, I don't think I could do anything you're doing. Just thinking about flying in a plane gives me the heebie geebies. I know!

I sound like an old fuddy-duddy, worrying like that.

We have a temporary pet squirrel. Unlike the baby bird we'd taken care of last year, this guy can't stay still. I think this one's going to have to stick around a bit longer, though. We think that when he fell out of the tree, he damaged his leg. It was three days before we could get him to eat.

He's a cute little thing. Never really thought about wild animals having any kind of personality but this critter is hysterical. Now that he's gotten used to us, if we don't feed him when he wants food he starts hopping around the cage. He'll talk to us the whole time we're eating dinner. And listen to this, this is too funny—when Mom has the radio on, he rocks back and forth to the music!

I hope this and the package reaches you before your birthday. I sent them separately like Uncle Popeye recommended. It seems to be working out well, so far.

Mom brought home some pictures of what the airplanes look like that you've been telling me about.

Didn't make me feel any better. I still worry that you're over there with the Japs shooting at you, and you're flying in one of those big clucky, scary things—and at night.

My friend Nancy's worried about her beau. She, nor her parents, haven't heard from him in over three months. I know she breathes a sigh of relief every day he's not on the list, and they haven't received the dreaded letter.

I keep praying. I just keep praying for everyone.

Well, off for now. Keep writing Harry and stay safe.

Best Regards,
Margaret

Letter Sixteen

End of November 1943

Dear Margaret,

Thank you for the card and books.

Your story about the squirrel's funny. We didn't have pets, weren't allowed to…but I do have a funny story to tell you that goes along with that.

When I was in seventh grade, my brother Mark, brought home a spider monkey that a friend of his couldn't keep any more. We kept it hidden in the basement for quite a few months.

Mom very rarely went down there. And I guess, when she did, Mark must've had the monkey with him because she never found out about him until it bit him.

I'll tell you what, that boy howled like he was dying! Mom came running down the stairs, saw the blood, saw the monkey, and that was the end of *that*.

By the end of the day, my brother had found a home for him. It was fun for a while, but I don't think I want another monkey as a pet…maybe a bird, something small like a parakeet.

To answer your question about Black Cats. We're just a PBY squadron who makes night flights. The PBYs are Catalinas…Cats. And they're painted a flat black so that we can fly at night and not be seen by the enemy.

Our insignia is a Black Cat. (I'll send a picture of it in the next letter. I haven't drawn one yet.)

I imagine it's pretty eerie for the Japs when we're near them. If it's cloudy, we'll use the clouds for cover and they can't see us. If it's not, we'll fly lower, closer to the water. When we fly close to the water, it is dangerous, but, they aren't looking down for us, they're looking up, so we have the clement of surprise.

Someone told me a while back the Japs thought we were a mysterious secret weapon because they couldn't see us.

We've been busy here in the South Pacific. The day after my birthday, October 11, on a preflight check, we found a gas leak. The only place that it could be fixed was at Ile Nou, New Caledonia.

While waiting for our plane to be fixed we had liberty in Noumea, New Caladonia. Living conditions were primitive. We stayed in tents.

A few days later, we moved to Halavo Bay RNZAF Base on Florida Island, in the Solomon Islands. (New Zealand Air Force) There's about fifteen PBY's operating from this base. This base was just across from Guadalcanal.

The living quarters weren't too bad as we were set up in the new Quonset Huts, and living conditions were pretty good.

For some reason they called this base Todd City. I haven't found out why yet.

From this point on things got away from being routine.

We made a Dumbo run to Rendova, (West of Guadalcanal), and picked up a marine Captain with two Japs he'd captured, and brought them back to base for interrogation.

This is the first time I saw the enemy up close. The Captain kept them in the bunk area. They had the most beautiful black eyes I ever saw.

The two never said a word. We didn't know if they understood English so there wasn't a lot of conversation going on until they were taken to the base.

They looked around plane, but mostly kept their eyes downward. When they did look at me, it was ever so briefly, and then they'd look away again.

The next day, we carried six New Zealander RADAR men to set up gear at Empress Augusta Bay. From there, we transported a Major and Captain of the Marines, and dropped them off at Treasury Island.

At Treasury Island, we transported another Marine Captain and Sergeant (SBD crew) who had lost their plane and dropped them off at Rendova.

November 24th, we moved from Todd City to the USS Coos Bay tender (AVP 25). The Coos Bay was a small tender and living conditions were crowded again. She was anchored in Halavo Bay, which was called Halavo Seaplane Base.

Yes, we did do a lot of hopping back and forth.

We took three officers and three enlisted men to Rendova where they plotted to lay buoys.

Then back to another Dumbo run to Empress Augusta Bay. We picked up three stretcher cases plus a Commander, Major, and three Lieutenants. With the eight of them in the seaplane, we made a quick transport to Vella Lavella which is northwest of Guadalcanal. We dropped off the injured there and then brought the officers back to Rendova.

While transporting them from the water launch to the plane I accidentally put my fingers in the bullet holes in one of the injured man's back.

He let me know about it. I felt bad, horrible really.

I wasn't thinking about anything except moving—we had to move, and we had to move fast.

While all this was going on the Japs were shelling us from shore. On most of these Dumbo hops we usually have air coverage so when we landed on the water we won't be sitting ducks.

There were a few night patrols toward Bougainville. We also did some spotting for DD's so they could lob shells onto the Island where the Japs were holed up.

At Halavo Bay we were still doing a lot of Dumbo runs, along with day and night patrols. We made a couple of runs to the Canal to drop passengers off, searched a sector that a B24 was supposed to have been ditched.

We also checked on a ship in distress, but she said they could make it back to the base.

During this time, there were a couple of close calls with unidentified planes. We were very glad to make it back.

We also ran into a couple of storms. I thought one of them was going to rip the wings off the plane.

That's how bad it was!

It felt like the time when I was with VP24 and we were tracking a hurricane and flew directly into the eye. Between the hurricanes and the instruments going wacky, sometimes it makes me wonder how we manage to limp back to home base.

You mentioned the '38 hurricane several months ago in a

letter. I do remember it all too well. That was rough.

My father had me, Don, and Mark take out his fishing boat. The four of us went around to all the houses to make sure everyone in the neighborhood was okay.

I sent gifts to everyone about a month ago. I don't know how long it'll take to get to you. I hope you get it in time.

Have a great holiday.

Keep writing!

Best Regards,
Harry

VPB 71 Black Cat Squadron
Black Eagle Crew

End of December 1943

Dear Harry,

Thank you for the Abalone necklace and bracelet. They're absolutely gorgeous! I have them on right now and have been showing them off to everyone.

I got a letter from Doris. Strangest thing. It looked like it'd been opened and read by someone before I got it. There were greasy finger and thumb prints on the page.

I know, considering the way Doris is, she would never have sent the letter out like that. I wonder why someone would feel so inclined to read her letters to me?

She just talked about being a waitress and how she'd never take for granted what waitresses have to do. She's got a whole different outlook on restaurant employees. She talked about the different people she's met and how she might go to France after the war.

Doris is still in Egypt and said she's planning on staying there for a while.

We heard on the radio that there's been more than a half million Nazi refugees coming to America since 1933. They said many of them are Jews…like Albert Einstein.

The newspaper and radio announcers broadcast information about a bunch of battles going on in the Solomon Islands. They mentioned some islands that you've talked about…Vella Lavella and Empress Augusta Bay.

Since I've practically memorized the map, I could picture in my head where all of these battles are taking place. And you in the thick of things!

Please be careful. I want you to come back home.

Best Regards,
Margaret

Letter Seventeen

End of March 1944

Dear Margaret,

I'm glad you like the necklace and bracelet. I was hoping you would. Thank you for the books and the set of colored pencils. It's a fine addition to the art supplies that you've sent before.

I'm not surprised that they're opening letters. Can't be too careful in a war, right?

The holidays came and went pretty quick, over before I realized it. You may have been watching for snowstorms, but, being here in the Southern Hemisphere, it's summertime and hot as Hades!

Yes, the Solomon Islands have been under some hefty fighting.

We had a temporary reprieve from fighting to celebrate and welcome 1944.

On February 19th, we moved from the Coos Bay to the USS Wright (AV 1). We've continued doing Patrols from Halavo.

As you can imagine, this moving around has been a pain. Anytime we wanted anything from our plane we had to get a boat and be transported. It was always hot and the planes were steaming. You have to realize also that we're pretty close to the Equator, too.

Also quinine's the pill of the day. Any problems, they give us quinine.

Well, I finally got my orders to go on leave! I plan on coming home! I'm so excited to be able to see you and my family. I'll make sure to give you better dates so I can pop over and visit!

About twenty of us were transported to the Canal on March 6th.

We took a DC-3 to Espirito overnight. A couple of days later we took a PBM-3 Pan-American to Funafuti. From Funafuti to Canton, Canton to Palmyra, Palmyra to Pearl. On our way to Pearl, we had an oil leak so we had to go back to Palmyra to have it fixed.

Started again this time and we made it to Pearl. Picked up a transport ship and landed in San Diego, California.

I haven't talked much about the guys (and they're a great group of guys to work with) so here's a list of the members of Crew 12.

PPC Lt. (jg) Cocks Calif., Lt. (jg) A.J. Lehmicke Minn., Lt. (jg) Nickolas Calif.

PC W. Kern ACMM Ill., E. Eaddy AMM1/c N.C., H. Lawrence ARM 1/c R.I., G. Saxton ARM 1/c Penn transferred new crew in July 1st radioman, M. Mikula ARM 2/c Ohio, transferred new crew in Oct 1st radioman., A. Miller ARM2/c Al. transferred new crew in February, J. Becker ARM 2/c Col., R. Byk AMM 1/c Mass., C. White AOM 1/c., R. Barnett AMM 2/c came aboard in December as Mech. Kern's was transferred out and E.I.Eaddy was made PC in December.

I have to tell you, crossing the Equator and International Date Line is a big deal.

We were issued Flight Crew Wings for enlisted men—this was new. This will be my first thirty-day leave since I left Newport on June 24, 1941.

Tour of overseas duty so far, twenty-eight months!

Looking forward to seeing you!

I'm coming home!

Best Regards,
Harry

May 1944

Dear Harry,

It was absolutely great seeing you while you were on leave. Dinner at your parents was killer-diller. I wish I had had more time to spend with you, but work does tend to get in the way.

Harry, you were so funny—especially when you were telling everyone about the gooney birds.

I thought your mother was going to pop you on the side of the head when you told us that you had to fix a cable on the seaplane and repaired it mid-flight.

I know your parents really didn't want to hear about the war stories, but I'm sure it was hard to do with all of the brothers together like that.

I don't think I've ever seen anyone pack down so many steamers, *linguiça*, or *chourico* in one sitting. I'm guessing you were missing the good food? Or was it that you were making up for the last couple of years?

Your dad is such a charmer. Now I know where you get it from. His English isn't too bad. I think he's just more comfortable speaking in his native tongue. We were able to have a decent conversation. A few Portuguese words thrown in here and there didn't hurt at all.

I told him that I didn't remember you being so tall, and he said that you were a little *fedelho* when you left and now you're taller than him. Mary told me later it means "squirt".

How was your trip to Long Island with your sister? Hope you had a great time. I adore her! She's one of my favorite people. And Van was great. I can see why they get along so well. I hope he didn't mind. I'm a really curious person and I was asking him all about the Squalus. I just find it completely fascinating.

I don't know how all of you do it. Listening to your stories, and your brothers, Van diving (with other rescuers) in the Momsen-McCann rescue chamber down 240 feet! It's just so scary to me.

Your family sure does have a lot of brave souls. Your mom was telling me about one of the boat trips they'd been taking back to come home from the Azores. I'm sure you've heard it several times. It was the one where she was coming back with the family, and Hap was a newborn, and they hit a storm.

Ack! I would've been crying my eyes out.

I want to travel and have some adventure but I don't think that's the kind I'll be looking for.

Well, Harry, it was great seeing you. Looking forward to your next, and hopefully final return home.

Please take care.

Best Regards,
Margaret

Letter Eighteen

July 1944

Dear Margaret,

I can't believe I was lucky enough to see Don while I was home. He's stationed in Norfolk, VA., now. I'm glad he made it home. As you know, Hap, who's in the Merchant Marines was also home. Of course, he came just in time for dessert!

To have almost all of us back together was more than I could've hoped for.

My dad's a hot-ticker, isn't he? He liked you, too.

Yes, I've heard the story about that trip. I guess it was the worst one. Most trips, according to Ma and Pop, were simple easy trips—long, but easy.

I haven't been to the Azores since I was sixteen. Pop wasn't too keen on going over there with all the problems hitting Europe, etc.

Doesn't matter how tall I get. I'll always be *fedelho* to my family, being the youngest and all. Either that or Horsepower, which Mark started calling me a few years ago and the rest of the family seemed to pick it up.

Mary and I went to Long Island to see my brother, Vic. He's working for Grumman Aircraft, and he gave me a tour of the plant he was working in, and other facilities within the company.

As Mary and I were on our way home to catch our train back to Providence, the taxi driver took us by the Empire State building. A couple of days before this a two engine bomber had run into the building and was still sticking out of one of the top floors.

At the end of June, after leave was over, my orders were to report back to HEDRON to North Island NAS, San Diego.

78

I think I mentioned it before. In May 1944, I transferred from HEDRON San Diego to VPB 71. They're flying PBY-5A's (Black Cats) amphibious. If you recall, Black Cats are painted all black, and most missions are flown at night.

I promised a picture of or insignia. It's enclosed.

There were a few changes in our radio equipment. Instead of one RU receiver, two new ARR receivers were installed. These new Super-Het receivers are much easier to use.

LORAN was also installed (long range navigation gear).

When we left the Hawaii area, it was useless as there were no LORAN station for us to use. RADAR's much better. We have antenna on each side of the forward hull that we can control.

Also, we've got the capability to install twin fifty canisters under each wing. They also installed twin thirties in our bow turret.

Our 50 calibers, in the right and left blisters now, had a large reservoir for our ammo between our guns attached to the walkway. This is so much better than the small one that was attached to the gun.

As far as clothing's concerned the only changes are a baseball cap, and a shoulder 38 caliber that was issued for us. Officers are now in flight suits.

We're told that we'll get flight suits later.

Most of our hops are bounces off water and mat. There were some instrument and familiarization hops. We also had simulated ditch exercises, where they dropped us into the pool.

We'd be fully dressed with a parachute harness on sitting in a chair. They dump us into the water, and we'd have to take our harness off and return to the surface.

Of course, we're monitored. A couple of sailors would be under water when we were dumped.

They also made us pass a swimming course. You'd be surprised how many of us didn't know how to swim!

Considering that I was born and raised on an island, all I could do was dog-paddle. You'd think I'd have learned how to swim sooner—considering I went to the beach every summer and we were surrounded by water!

We were issued 38s, and out to the range we went. At the range we had target shooting with the 38s and 45s, rapid and slow.

We've been doing more intense training missions, bounce RADAR, navigation, V flight, night formation, night bounce, and gunnery. Finally after all that, we started flying with our own pilots and crew.

Dear Margaret,

I've put this in an envelope a couple of times to mail to you and I kept adding things. Sorry it's so long.
Have a great summer.

Best Regards,
Harry

Letter Nineteen

August 1944

Dear Margaret,

Hope you're feeling better by the time this reaches you. Mom's letter came last week and she mentioned that you got a summer Flu.

This is more of a continuation from the last letter. We've been all over lately, flying with our own crew and plane.

We're still doing familiarization hops. Except for one night bounce, our front nose wheel collapsed on landing. Absolutely no one was hurt.

Our twin 50s, which was new, was installed under the wing have been working fine. Also, we've had some practice doing torpedo runs and high altitude bombing.

We made a forced landing in Ensenada, Mexico on a small fighter strip for personal supplies for our trip south. We had to make a trip into town.

It took a while to get the aircraft squared away. It was quite a take-off as we had to run the engines at high speed, when we were ready to take off both pilots released the brakes which gave us the speed to take off.

We also started advice training flights, fighter evasive action, low attitude bombing, anti-submarine action with live depth charges, and using our new 50 caliber wing guns.

Preparing for flight to Hawaii, we had an extra rubberized tank installed in the bunk department. This gave us more fuel to reach Hawaii. I may not have mentioned this before, we also had one of these tanks in our wing section.

For our trip to Hawaii, we had extra passengers and our gear

Dear Margaret,

plus records etc. The flight took us 19.3 hours to Hilo which was a short stop, and 1.5 hours to Kaneohe, our home base.

We've got more training. I'll close this for now. Hope you're getting better.

Best Regards,
Harry

End of September 1944

Dear Harry,

Thank you for your concern. I am feeling much better. It was a pretty rough there for a while. Even Mom was worried. I swear my bones hurt for weeks after the flu was gone!

We went to the Hampton's for a week. We haven't gone anywhere since the war started. I think all of us needed a break.

We got hit with a pretty hefty hurricane, right after we got back from vacation. They're calling it the Great Atlantic Hurricane. It wasn't as bad as the '38 hurricane but we still had some damage. Not to us personally, but neighbors lost roofs, water damage, downed trees, etc.

I'm still volunteering at the Red Cross and we were very busy. I was able to work more hours with them since the restaurant was closed. (No electricity)

My aunt's house got water damage from a hole in the roof. They think a tornado touched down, shearing off the top of the tree in their front yard. It landed on the roof, piercing a hole in it when it landed.

Your birthday present will be late. Sorry! I didn't have a hurricane or the flu on my "to do" list so I wasn't expecting any delays.

I'm glad everything worked out on your flights and you made it safely back to Hawaii. With everything you're doing it would've been ironic if you got hurt because your own plane's front wheel broke off.

You know, I sit here and read everything you're telling me, but I don't think it really sank in until your last couple of letters. I read about the fifty calibers, the thirties, RADAR, codes, the bombs, and all that you're doing—Black Cat night flights, bombing enemy ships, prowling in the night. It's terrifying.

My uncle was telling me that you have to strap the bombs up with pulleys, and attach them on the underside of the wings. He explained that you guys go to the bomb dump and use a small crane to lift the 250 lb. bombs. He said the tailspin is put on manually and tightly. Uncle Popeye was very adamant on how important that was. I bet it's fascinating using the pulleys to attach the bomb under those wings. Now that my mother gave me pictures of the PBYs, I can get a better idea of what you're flying in.

So, I'm guessing that since patrol airboats weren't originally made for bombing, that's why they have to be strapped on under the wings?

I'm learning, slowly but surely.

Not much else is happening here. Please take care.

Best Regards,
Margaret

Letter Twenty

End of December 1944

Dear Margaret,

I received your gifts for my birthday and Christmas on the same day. I opened my birthday present and love the books!

I'll be honest. I didn't open my Christmas gift until Christmas. I was tempted, but I wanted to wait. The sketch pads are great.

Thank you for both gifts.

To give you a catch-up of what we've been doing:

From mid-September to the day after my birthday, we were doing continuous training at Kaneohe Naval Air Station. Then we did advance duty at Midway until November, which is most likely why I hadn't received any mail.

Most of the time we were flying patrols from Midway. We lost one of our planes out there. They were later picked up, but we lost of the two men.

I know we're supposed to focus on how many lives we've saved and helped, but when we lose someone it's hard to shake it off.

Nothing changed here except we had a mess hall to chow down in. No fancy dinners here, not like the holiday dinners we had a few years ago.

Living arrangements were tents, but now, we have a shower setup we could use.

After Midway we continued training.

Mid-November, we're finally on our way and haven't stopped.

First hop to Johnston then to Kwajalein, trained in

Kwajalein for 3 days.

From Kwajalein to Manus then to Owi. We had four days rest there.

Owi to Biak and returned back to Owi.

Owi to Moratai, Netherlands East Indies. At Moratai, we were all living in tents. Things were a little crude. Moratai's a small island south of the Philippines in the Netherlands East Indies Group, and all operations were conducted off the water—working the liberation of the Philippines. This'll be our home base for a while.

We were issued China-Burma patches to put on our jackets. Trouble was, it was too hot to wear jackets. Therefore, we didn't do it.

We've had a couple of eventful flights.

Late November, on the 26th, we were in a night flight that lasted 14 hours. We bombed, strafed, and sank a medium-sized enemy freighter-transport (Fox Tare Charlie) west of Jolo Island in the Sulu Archipelago.

Making effective use of land cover, Lt. Turner scored two direct hits with 250lb bombs, following which he made a strafing run, raking the vessel with our four .50 caliber wing guns, and twin thirties.

The target was seen to blow up, and when the plane returned for further observation, it'd disappeared. Anti-aircraft fire from shore gun positions, and one on the ship was received during the attack.

A couple of weeks later, on December 6th, we had a night flight that ended up lasting about 15 hours. Cmdr. Gillette led a flight of three planes on a mission to attack shipping in the harbor at Balikpapan, Borneo.

In spite of unfavorable weather all three planes reached the Borneo coast in the vicinity of Balikpapan but were unable to complete their attack because of weather conditions over the target area.

While negotiating a mountain pass in the Celebes under instrument conditions. Lt. Turner felt his starboard wing strike a hard but yielding object throwing the plane into a left down wing position.

Lt. Turner asked me to get on the RADAR which was fired up but on standby. Putting the plane into a steep climb, we kept up a running conversation until I started seeing a clear signal under the noise pattern.

I told him he could level off, which he did. At this point, the plane had a slight vibration so we continued on with our mission. After returning to base we found under examination the plane revealed a damaged wingtip float and starboard running light as well as two deep indentations in the leading edge of the starboard wing well outboard and several rips in the fabric on the underside.

Several sizable wood fragments were found wedged in the leading edge of the wing and near the wing tip float. We concluded that we must have hit the top of the trees on the side of the mountain.

We were lucky, very lucky!

A few days later, on Dec. 9th, we had a shorter hop (about 9.8 hours). We were searching for Lt. (jg) Shelley's plane which failed to return from patrol. Shelley Lt. (jg), Auburn AOMB2c, and Art Breslin ARM 2c, who was from Providence, were both killed in the crash. The rest of the crew was reported to be in the hands of friendly guerrillas.

We had another memorable night flight on December 11th. (12.5 hours). Sandakan Borneo, we bombed and strafed shipping. Of the six 250lbs G.P. (general purpose) bombs dropped, one was seen to hit and sink a lugger, and two direct hits were made on the docks.

A second lugger was sunk by strafing.

Except for the losses on the last Dumbo run for the downed plane, we've had a few good, successful runs.

On December 28th, we left Moratai and arrived in Owi for some much needed R &R. We're scheduled to go to Moratai in a few days and I wanted to get this letter out to you while I could.

Take care. Hope you had a great holiday.

Best Regards,
Harry

Dear Margaret,

Mid-December 1944

Dear Harry,

It sure is getting hot over there for you. Please be safe! I keep you in my prayers every day.

With everything that you're doing, it's so hard to tell you my simple, everyday happenings. What you're doing is so dangerous, and my little world is safe because of brave men like you. I hope you know how much everyone appreciates what you and our servicemen are doing for us.

The radio and newspapers have blasted the liberation of the Philippines. They're saying that taking the Philippines back will help us beat the Japs. My uncle said he heard they used battleships from Pearl Harbor, raised from the mud as a trap. What an ingenious idea! He said the Japs losses were huge.

And you were a part of it all!

Did you see General MacArthur when he was there?

They announced last month that the Japs lost Guam, too. And I'm guessing you already know that since you're in the thick of things over there.

There was a spot on the radio about Glenn Miller. He's MIA. He was taking a plane from England to Paris and never arrived. His music will live on. I know it will.

There's a lot of famous entertainers who've joined in the war effort. Jimmy Stewart, Joe DiMaggio, Jackie Coogan, Henry Fonda are a few I can think of right now.

It's heating up over in Europe just like in the Pacific. Since D-Day and taking back France, the tide's definitely turning to our advantage. The news said that the Battle of Bulge was a crucial win. There're rumors that what the Germans are doing is worse than what's being reported, and that the SS massacred POWs.

They say the Japs are worse. I hope not!

Uncle Popeye said if you were captured and the Japs knew you were a radioman, they'd be even rougher on you.

I cried myself to sleep! I'm getting choked up right now just thinking about it.

I know you can't tell me a lot, except the stuff that's already happened…"Loose lips sink ships" and all, but I'm glad that you're keeping me posted with what you can tell me.

Well, thank goodness the election is over! It's no surprise that FDR won. Even though Mom didn't vote for Dewey, she says that they'll probably put term limits on the presidency to avoid one man having too much control.

Take care.

Best Regards,
Margaret

Letter Twenty-one

March 1945

Dear Margaret,

This letter is going to be more "diary-ish" and detailed than anything else. For some reason, I feel like I need to write all of this down. We've been full speed ahead and everything is becoming a big blurr.

I have to admit, if I'd had any time off, the only thing I've wanted to do is sleep.

The first few months of 1945 have been just as busy as the last few months of '44.

January 4, 1945: Moratai to USS Tangier AV-8 at Leyte Gulf, Luzon, Philippines. We're living aboard ship.

January 6: We've had night flights. We were in the air about 15 hours. We were covering a large convoy which was moving from Leyte to Lingayen Gulf, protecting them from possible enemy submarine contacts and bogeys.

Being Black Cats, we had to keep moving so the enemy couldn't find us. By January 12th, we were living aboard USS Barataria AVP-33 which is a small sea plane tender. Our new flights were now targeting the west coast of Formosa, and the China coast.

For some reason I forgot to add this into my notes. On January 22nd, a 12.8 hour night flight, we bombed the heavily fortified Mako Island, Pescadores.

We made a single run at low altitude and put four 250lb G.P bombs, and two 100lb incendiary clusters squarely on the barracks, shops, and warehouses without having any return fire. The initial concussion of the bombs was followed by a series of explosions and large fires.

We had another long night flight (13.1hrs) on January 29th. At Ishigaki Harbor in the Sakashima group, we sighted an old type Jap destroyer and two DE's. As we were making our run, we broke off because of heavy light and medium AA, anti-aircraft attacks.

We were flying on the west coast of Formosa near Tainan when a small Jap freighter was sighted (SC). Due to bad weather we had to make RADAR approaches. Taking over the RADAR, we made three approaches before we made visual contact.

Once we had visual, we dropped two 500lb bombs. This was also a 12.8 hour night flight. (February 1st) Making another run on RADAR, we then dropped our other two 500lb bombs. After that, we came back for a strafing run.

By this time the ship was already taking water. We continued to search with RADAR, and failed to re-establish any contact with the vessel.

The next day was a bit rough on all of us. A Black Cats crew, crew 14: Lt. (jg) Albert John Lehmicke, Jr. and crew 14 (Charles H. White ACOM) went out on a mission but never returned. I flew with them in VP 71.

All of them, gone.

More night flights have kept us searching the coast. On February 16th, a 12.8 hour flight, we were patrolling along the west coast of Formosa, I made RADAR contact—three blips on the radar screen.

Visibility was very poor and we made multiple runs before we could make visual contact. Mr. Turner concentrated most of his effort on the larger ship which was a Tare Baker class.

We spent over three hours making multiple runs with Radar before we could get visual, expending all our bombs and ammo before we left the area.

The Tare Baker was motionless in the water and down slightly by the stern. The two Sugar Charlies (enemies) left during the early part of the encounter.

February 20: Night Flight, 13 hours. We changed our search pattern around this time to include the China coast. We made a search of Amoy Harbor, Negat. On our return to base, we bombed a RADAR Station on the southern tip of Formosa.

On February 22nd, we landed at Clark Field, and had a

chance to have a two-day liberty in Manila, Philippines.

Back to work on February 24th for another 12.5 hour night flight on the China coast of Swatow, Negat.

This was one of those really dark nights—a serious advantage for us since our plane is painted a flat black. I don't know if I told you this or not, but depending on the night, depends on how we fly. If there are clouds, we use the clouds for cover. The enemy can't spot us.

If there aren't any clouds to use for cover, we fly low. The enemy, if they hear us, is looking up and misses us. We have the element of surprise.

This night stands out for me. I picked up blip on RADAR and had Lt. Turner make a run but just before release he made out a lighthouse.

That was too close for comfort! On the return, we bombed the barracks at Pescadores.

Another night flight (12 hours) on February 28th, we patrolled the China Coast, Swataw to Amoy Harbor, and then over to Pescadores.

Observing ships in the Mako harbor, Turner was flying low at 150 feet. We were making a run on a Sugar Baker when we encountered return fire.

We dropped two 500lb bombs and a 250lb bomb. With the intense fire that resulted from the drops, we couldn't see if we'd made a hit.

Two men, Chief Smith, who was using the bow twin 30's was hit in the leg, and PC Reardon, at his station in the tower, was also hit in the leg.

We were all ducking the flying shrapnel, the projectiles were just as dangerous and hazardous as the bullets.

As we were pulling out of our run, Lt. Turner dropped the rest of our bombs on unidentified buildings.

On the trip back to the base, I was now acting as radioman sending messages and also working the RADAR. On the RADAR, we had a bogie following us for a while, but he didn't fire upon us.

When we returned to Lingayen Gulf, we beached our aircraft and got the men aboard the ship. Chief Smith lost part of his leg.

We realized how lucky we were when, later, during routine

inspection and assessment of the plane, they counted 65 holes in the hull.

Somebody upstairs was protecting us, both engines were fine.

Now that I'm here, everything that happened is sinking in. I'm wound-up and exhausted all at the same time. I'd love to be able to shoot off some steam right now, but that's not going to happen.

Too close…too close for comfort this time.

I want to sign off for now, along with sending your birthday present. I hope you have a wonderful birthday!

Best Regards,
Harry

Dear Margaret,

Beginning of May 1945

Dear Harry,

Holy Cow! I read your letter and started shaking. I was terrified and angry. My heart was thundering in my chest.

You're going to laugh, but I was appalled that they fought back. My reaction was "How dare they?!"

I know, silly of me.

I've gotten another job. Mom broke her wrist and is out of work, so it's a temporary job. I'm working at Mr. Williams' butcher shop. He's working around my schedule at LaForge, and understands that it's only temporary. He was very generous to help us out.

As far as I'm concerned, he's got a loyal customer for life. I know he didn't need any more hired help, and he gave me a job anyway.

Saw the movie, *The Enchanted Cottage* with Robert Young and Dorothy McGuire. It's a romantic movie so you probably aren't interested in watching anything like that.

Nancy and I loved it. It was a really good movie. I think Robert Young is such a sheik!

Well, off I go. The alarm went off and I need to get ready for work.

Be careful, Harry. I want to see your charming smile, again when you come back home.

Best Regards,
Margaret

Letter Twenty-two

End June 1945

Dear Margaret,

At the beginning of March, we started living at Jinamoc Island. Making a few patrols from Jinamoc, we had no enemy contacts.

We also made several small hops to Samar, Tacloban. It's in the eastern Visayas region of the Philippines.

Liberty!

Clark Field, liberty in Manila, Nichols Field.

We had to make some repairs to the plane and on March 29th we had a test flight. We're back in commission.

A few days later on 31st we moved to Samar Island. We did a patrol from Samar tracking a typhoon.

April, May, and June, we were pretty much doing the same old stuff, typical all day hops averaging about thirteen hours, doing Dumbo runs, patrols, etc.

We made a patrol covering an English DD which had been hit. We've covered a couple of army strikes; one at Suluan Point, and also at Negros.

I was discharged from VPB 71 on June 14th and will receive my next duty assignment while on leave.

Yes, you read it right. I'm coming home!

It'll be a long and interesting trip.

First, it'll be from Samar to Guam R5D, then from Guam to Kwajalein. From Kwajalein, we go to Johnson and Johnson we head to Kaneohe Air Station, Hawaii.

I left for the States on June 22, 1945 aboard the USS General R.E.Callen (AP139). I arrived at Naval Air Station

Dear Margaret,

Alameda, California on June 28th, and will be sending this letter out today.

I'll be heading to Rhode Island for a thirty day leave. I'm coming home!

Looking forward to seeing you and my family.

Best Regards,
Harry

Letter Twenty-three

August 1945

Dear Margaret,

I arrived back to the West Coast after being home on leave for thirty days. I was assigned to duty station in Alameda in the San Francisco Bay area. This is a huge facility. Someone told me there over 29,000 personnel.

It feels really good to be on American land.

We just got the announcement!!

The war is over! I will thank Colonel Paul Tibbets, his Enola Gay, and celebrate August 14th for the rest of my life.

I have the chance to get out on points received.

I think, at this time, I realize that this was enough.

Thank you for being a pen pal all these years. Hearing news from home was always a pleasure.

I appreciate your warm wishes and your tolerance for my long-winded letters.

Looking forward to seeing you again when I arrive home.

Best Regards,
Harry

Dear Margaret is a product of the author's imagination. The letters never existed.

However…It *is* based on a true story.

Chief ARM Henry Lawrence was awarded the Distinguished Flying Cross, 3 Air Medals, Navy Unit Citation, Philippine Liberation Medal, and Air Crew wings with three stars. He returned home as Chief ARM. He was authorized a total of seven stars on his Asian Pacific Ribbon. He was also recommended for the Silver Star, but that was not awarded.

Dear Margaret is based on the true life WW2 experiences of Chief ARM Henry Lawrence—a Pearl Harbor survivor, Black Cat, and decorated war veteran. It is written with as much historical accuracy of the events of that time period.

After the war, Henry Lawrence spent another eighteen years in the Navy Reserves, leaving the service as a Master Chief Petty Officer.

Most letters from Margaret are true historical events involving relatives and friends from her side of the family. They are as accurate as the author could portray them.

All letters to Margaret have been taken from Mr. Lawrence's memoirs. If you would like to read Mr. Lawrence's original memoirs, *I Was Just a Radioman* is available on Amazon as an e-book or in print at your favorite bookstore.

WITH FOUR SONS EACH IN SERVICE

These Newport mothers are, left to right, Mrs. Jennie E. Brawner of 1 West Howard street, Mrs. Mary S. Lawrence of 18 Dearborn street, and Mrs. Luiza Furtado of 20 Willow street. The women attended the recent dedication exercises at the Roll of Honor at the city hall.   —Kerschner Photo.

VPB 71 Black Cat Squadron
Black Eagle Crew

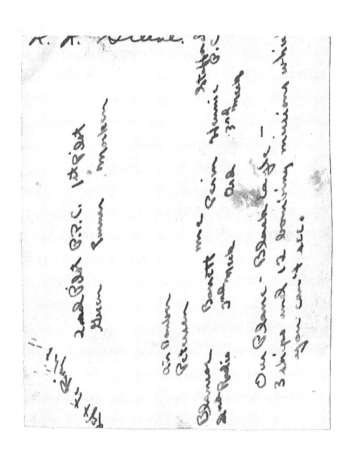

103

Insigna Designed by
Milton Caniff

UNITED STATES FLEET
FLEET AIR WING SEVENTEEN

F39/(02-ka)

Serial: 1233

31 December 1944

From: The Commander, Fleet Air Wing SEVENTEEN.
To : The Commanding Officer, Patrol Bombing Squadron 71.

Subject: Display of Insignia in Recognition of Destruction
to Enemy Surface Vessel.

Reference: (a) CinCPacFlt ltr. 511-44 dated 25 Sept. 1944.

1.   In recognition of sinking one Japanese FTC,
06-00 N 121-40 E, on 27 November by crew number 8, you are
hereby authorized to paint the prescribed insignia on your
assigned aircraft, or its replacement, while in the squadron.

2.   Crew:

Lieut. A.O. TUSKER
Lieut.(jg) O.L. MOKER
Ensign R.E. GREENE

PETERSEN, N.J.   ACM2c
BLENDER, H.A.   ACM3c
LAWRENCE, H.F.   ACM1c
KEARDON, L.E.   ACM2c
BARGHTT, G.A.   ARM3c
FERIN, O.W.   ACM1c

O. B. JONES

Black Cat Stamp VPB 71

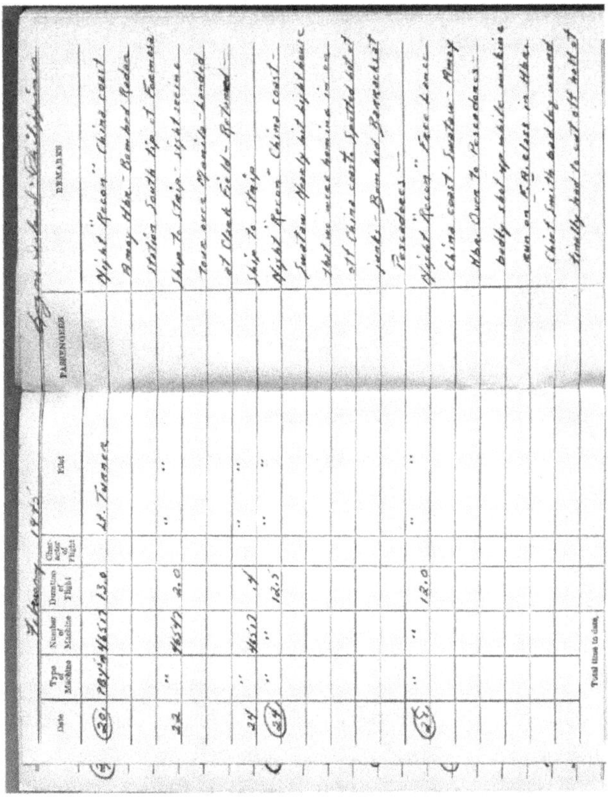

Random Page
Flight Log Book

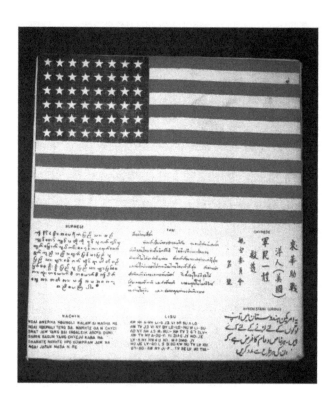

American Flag with Pacific
Area Languages

美國空軍來華助戰仰我軍民一體救護

國民政府航空委員會

借用字第 W 54153 號

Chinese Flag WW II

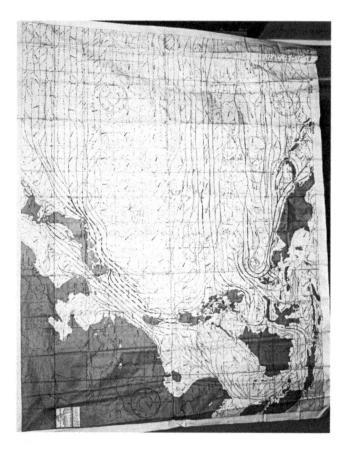

Silk Survival Map
Pacific Ocean

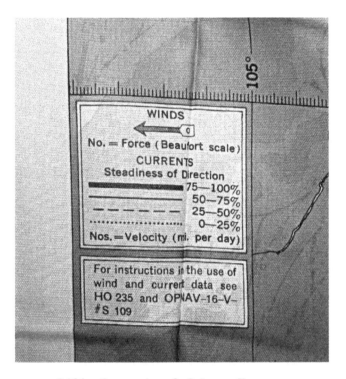

Silk Survival Map Inset

HENRY P. LAWRENCE
GETS FLYING CROSS

Chief Radioman Cited for Aerial Flight During Operations Against Japs

Henry P. Lawrence, aviation chief radioman, U. S. N.R., son of Mr. and Mrs. Anthony C. Lawrence of 18 Dearborn street, has received the Distinguished Flying Cross for achievement in aerial flight during operations in the Southwestern Pacific, First Naval District headquarters in Boston has announced

The citation accompanying the award to Lawrence, who has been in the service five years, and signed by Secretary of the Navy James V. Forrestal, acting in behalf of President Truman, states the Newporter earned the decoration for heroism and extraordinary achievement in aerial flight as an air-crewman during operations against Japanese forces from December 18, 1944, to February 1, 1945. Participating in 20 combat missions over hostile territory in the vicinity of enemy operational airfields, the citation continues, Lawrence rendered valuable service to his pilot, thereby contributing to the success of his plane.

Henry P. Lawrence
(on the right)
Receiving the Distinguished
Navy Cross

Margaret and Harry Lawrence
June 4, 1951